AN ECSTASY OF BONES
a serial killer thriller

WREN DELACROIX, BOOK THREE

V. J. Chambers

Punk Rawk Books

THE BONE FOREST
© 2019 by V. J. Chambers
www.vjchambers.com

Punk Rawk Books

All characters appearing in this work are fictitious. Any resemblance to real persons, living or dead, is purely coincidental.

All rights reserved. No part of this book may be used or reproduced in any manner whatsoever without written permission except in the case of brief quotations embodied in critical articles and reviews

ISBN: 9781689780902
Printed in the United States of America
10 9 8 7 6 5 4 3 2 1

AN ECSTASY OF BONES

a serial killer thriller

WREN DELACROIX, BOOK THREE

V. J. Chambers

CHAPTER ONE

Wren Delacroix stepped across the threshold of the Daily Bean, the coffee shop in Cardinal Falls where she began each day. She had noted that Detective Caius Reilly's car was in the parking lot, which meant that he was likely to have bought her a coffee already, and she wondered what it would be.

Wren didn't like repeats when it came to coffee. She liked new flavors, new combinations, exciting things. So, typically, Reilly would buy her whatever the barista Angela James recommended. Angela liked Wren, because she considered her the coffee shop's own private taste tester, so Angela could try anything she wanted out on Wren, and Wren would try it.

Actually, today, Angela was probably hoping to get some feedback on the toasted coconut mocha she'd made for Wren yesterday.

Reilly was at the counter, ordering drinks. Maliah Wright was next to him. She was craning her neck up to look all around the interior of the Daily Bean. She'd never been here before, Wren guessed.

Maliah worked with Wren and Reilly at the tri-state task force. She was the computer specialist, handling anything that involved the internet or technology. She and Reilly were also having an affair, one that they both seemed to deny that they were having. But now, look at them here, together, getting coffee.

Where the hell was Maliah's husband?

Because Maliah was still married. Reilly had been married, too, when they'd started hooking up, but now he was divorced, and the fact that the two of them kept up this relationship...

Well, Wren probably shouldn't judge, what with the fact that she was in some kind of complicated sex-buddy thing with the guy she'd had a crush on when she was a teenager. Whatever it was that was going on with Hawk, she couldn't bring herself to call it a relationship, even though she knew that he wanted more from her than what he was getting.

Wren had come through the door briskly, a woman on a mission, but now she stopped dead and looked at Reilly and Maliah.

Maliah noticed her. "Oh, Delacroix," she said. She turned and touched Reilly. "Cai, she's here, you don't have to order her anything."

Reilly turned from the counter to Wren. "Hey, Wren." He grinned at her widely.

Wren sucked in a breath, plastering a big smile on her face. She made her way over to Maliah and then looked down at the other woman's hand. She wasn't wearing her wedding ring. Hmm.

"Hey, Wren," said Angela brightly. "What you do you think about a bananas foster cafe au lait today?"

"Sounds great," said Wren, who was still looking at Maliah's naked finger on her left hand.

Maliah made a noise in the back of her throat.

Wren, who realized she hadn't greeted her, whipped her gaze up to meet Maliah's. "Good morning," she said, too brightly.

Maliah pursed her lips.

Wren lifted her chin.

Reilly cleared his throat. "Uh, how'd you sleep?"

"Great," said Wren. She arched an eyebrow. "You?"

Reilly scratched the back of his neck, looking away. He laughed to himself. "Yeah, that was a dumb question."

"So, you guys are out in public together and everything," said Wren.

"I'm separated," snapped Maliah.

"Oh," said Wren, and it was like a bucket of cold water had been thrown over her head. "Well, then… great. That's great for, um, you two."

"Thanks," said Reilly, slinging an arm around Maliah. "See you at the office."

"Yeah," said Wren, giving him a little salute. She watched as they walked out of the coffee shop with their coffees.

The door closed behind them.

Angela poured milk into a cup and stirred. "So, what did you think of the mocha from yesterday?"

"It was amazing," said Wren quietly.

"You didn't think it was too heavy on the coconut?"

Wren shook her head. "No. It was perfect. Really perfect."

Angela dumped brewed coffee in with the milk. "You're probably distracted with this case. I hear that there's already a new killer in Cardinal Falls."

"Yeah," muttered Wren. Everything to do with that was crazy.

"It's like we're cursed, I swear," said Angela. She topped the drink off with whipped cream and sprinkles of shaved chocolate. Then she set it on the counter.

"That looks delicious," said Wren.

"Hope you like it."

"What do I owe you?"

"Six even."

Wren dug money out of her pocket and put it on the counter. Then she picked up her drink. She tasted it and shut her eyes. Ah, the heaven of caffeine in the morning. Perfect.

* * *

When Wren got to headquarters, Reilly wasn't in his office.

She figured he was in Maliah's office, but she wasn't sure she wanted to go in there. They wouldn't be, like, making out at work, right? That would be totally unprofessional. She couldn't picture Reilly doing something like that. He was pretty much a stickler for rules.

Or was he?

He'd lied for her when she'd shot Kyler Morris, after all. And there was the fact that she worked here at all. He had hired her using discretionary funds allocated to him for consulting experts. She wasn't even an expert, not really. She hadn't finished at the FBI Academy. She'd dropped out.

She wanted to talk to him, but maybe she'd just wait until he was done with Maliah, with whatever they were doing. Just to be safe.

But then she heard Reilly's laughter coming from Maliah's office, and she noticed the door was open.

She decided to risk it. She went down the hallway and stopped outside Maliah's door.

Reilly was leaning against the wall, drinking his coffee. Maliah was sitting on her desk chair, her legs crossed toward him. They were both laughing.

Wren felt awkwardly as though she should start laughing too, but she didn't know why they were laughing. She couldn't do that. She just stood there.

Reilly noticed her. "Oh, hey, Wren, what's up?"

"I wanted to talk to you," she said. "You know how that last case we had, it turned out that Noah Adams wasn't really a serial killer, he was just trying to hide the fact that he'd killed his girlfriend?"

"Yeah?" said Reilly.

"Well, it occurs to me that this thing with Oliver Campbell, it's only one body. Even though he was posed just like the victims of Major Hill, that doesn't mean that this is part of a serial case."

Reilly considered this. "You know, you're right."

"I am?" said Wren.

Reilly nodded. "I mean, we still got our hands full tying up the Noah Adams case. This *is* only one body right now. It's not really our jurisdiction."

* * *

"You've got to be kidding me," said Chief Andrew Thomas. He was standing behind his desk at the Cardinal Falls Police Station. He was wearing a suit and tie, but his tie had a strange yellow stain on the end of it. Maybe mustard. "You think my department has the resources to work this case? Hell, the entire reason the task force was created was because we couldn't do it fifteen years ago."

"Well, this isn't a serial case," said Reilly.

"Like hell it's not," said Thomas. "The body was posed like all those other bodies."

"Yeah," said Wren, "but they were all female and between the ages of nine and thirteen. This is a grown man. It doesn't fit the profile."

"Not to mention," said Reilly, "we already locked the killer up."

"So, it's someone completely different," said Wren.

"Well, maybe," said Thomas.

"Maybe?" said Reilly.

"There's a possibility you locked up the wrong guy," said Thomas. He eyed Wren. "I was surprised you put away one of your own anyway."

"One of my own?" said Wren. "What are you talking about?"

"You members of the Fellowship, you stick together is all," said Thomas.

"I'm not a member of the Fellowship," said Wren.

"Well," said Thomas, "close enough."

"Come on, Lieutenant," said Reilly. "Why don't you put someone from your office on it, see what they can dig up?"

"And when another body drops, then we turn all our information over to you so that you can take credit for our hard work?" said Thomas. "I don't think so. This is a task force case, and you need to put tax dollars to good use and start working it yourselves."

"Maybe someone had a grudge against Oliver," said Wren. "Maybe someone wanted revenge against him. After all, he had a penchant for violence."

"What?" said Thomas. "Why would you say that?"

Wren pressed her lips together. The truth was that Oliver Campbell was her half brother. He'd told her that when he'd captured her and stuck her down in an old well for safekeeping. He was going to forcibly extract her bone marrow so that Wren could donate it to his sister, who was dying of leukemia. But she had decided not to press charges against her brother after she got free. She had decided that she would let it go, since she was free.

And then Oliver had turned up dead.

Heck, maybe she should come clean with Thomas. If she did, maybe she could beg off working the case since she was related to the victim.

Of course, that probably wouldn't fly here in Cardinal Falls, which was a small community and where lots of people were related. That would make things too hard for the department to enforce if no one ever worked a case with someone they were related to. It wasn't feasible.

Besides, she didn't have sisterly emotions for Oliver. She mostly hated him for capturing her.

Given time, she might have come around to pressing charges. Right after it happened, however, she'd been too busy trying to recover to want to go through another ordeal. She still had bruises from where she'd jumped out of a moving car trying to get away from Oliver.

"No reason," Wren muttered.

Reilly eyed her.

She looked away.

"You're not going to take the case?" said Reilly.

"It's not our case," said Thomas. "It's yours."

"Well, if we take it, our priority is going to be tying up

loose ends on the last case we wrapped, not this investigation, not yet."

"That's bullshit," said Thomas.

"You can't give up one guy to go ask around and see if Oliver Campbell had any enemies?" said Reilly.

"He did," said Thomas. "Those crazies up at the compound. They killed his daddy, didn't they? And now, look how they laid out his body. They killed him too."

Wren folded her arms over her chest. "You know, this is exactly why I don't trust this department to do anything right. This kind of ineptitude and prejudice. It was never the Fellowship that killed anyone, it was only—"

"Your mama?" said Thomas.

Wren drew in a breath, trying to steady herself. She didn't feel steady.

Reilly put a hand on her shoulder. "What my associate is trying to say—"

"What I'm trying to say is that we wouldn't let you touch this case if you were the last police department on earth," said Wren in an icy voice. "Of course we'll work it. That's the only way justice is ever going to be done."

And then she peeled Reilly's hand off her shoulder and stalked out of Thomas's office, slamming the door behind her on her way out.

CHAPTER TWO

When Wren got out to Reilly's car, it was locked, so she stood there like an idiot next to the passenger side, fuming, angry at herself for losing her cool, angry that she'd somehow managed to volunteer to take another case that might not even be a serial killer—

But no.

There was another reason why she didn't want to work this case, and the reason was swimming around in her subconscious, and she refused to look at it, to face it down. She couldn't let that thought surface. She simply could not.

Reilly appeared several minutes later, twirling his car keys on his forefinger.

"Unlock the fucking door already," she snarled.

He raised his eyebrows and used the key to unlock her side first. He didn't have a key fob with a clicker because he'd lost it, so he had to unlock the car manually.

She hurled herself into the car and busied herself with the seatbelt.

Reilly got in next to her.

She slammed the seatbelt into place.

Reilly put the keys in the ignition.

She looked at him.

He sat back in his seat, waiting.

"I'm sorry," she said.

"Yeah," he said.

"Oh, come on, we both know we were going to end up working this case, anyway. We want to work this case, don't we? If we don't, then what's going to happen to the task force? They could disband us, right? We need cases to, you know, exist."

He turned the key in the ignition and backed up the car.

They pulled out of the parking lot and drove in silence for several moments.

Wren started talking again. "How hard could it be, anyway? You did great with the case once you knew that Noah Adams wasn't a serial killer. So, this will be the same thing. We'll make a list of people who had a grudge against Oliver."

"Well, it occurs to me that you might top that list at the moment," said Reilly.

"Me?" Her voice was shrill. "I thought we left this idea that I was guilty behind already. You're not seriously accusing me, are you?"

He glanced at her. "Not you, no. But we had another suspect for Major's murders. You said he was our best suspect more than once, and—"

"Stop," said Wren. "Stop it, now."

"Wren, I distinctly remember you saying that you didn't want to press charges against Oliver, and him being all, 'He needs to face consequences.' I don't know his exact words, but it was something like that."

Wren squeezed her eyes shut. "No," she said. "No, no, no."

"For what it's worth," said Reilly. "I respect the guy. He had my back when I went after Colt Baldwin. He, uh, he... well, we might not have gotten out of there without him. But the guy he's..."

"Creepy?" said Wren. "He said you called him that."

"I know you don't want to think your boyfriend is—"

"He's not my boyfriend!" She nearly screamed it.

Reilly flinched. "Okay."

Wren rubbed her forehead. "Sorry."

"It's all right," said Reilly.

"He was with me," said Wren. "The night that Oliver was killed, he was with me."

It was quiet again.

Wren had almost used this alibi for Hawk before, back with Jenny Smith, but she'd known that it was possible that Hawk could have gotten out of bed with her, while she was sleeping, without waking her. Maybe not likely, but possible, so she hadn't fessed up to the alibi. Also, she'd been embarrassed to admit she was sleeping with Hawk, but now that ship had sailed, and Reilly knew.

"Okay," said Reilly finally. "Okay. He's got an alibi. Fine."

Now it was quiet again, and the silence was uncomfortable and weighty. She rested her head against the window and shut her eyes.

"This is the reason you wanted it out of our laps, though, right?" said Reilly. "Even with that alibi, you knew that it looked like he might have—"

"No." She turned to him.

"Did you tell Hawk about the crime scenes?" said Reilly. "Did you tell him what Major did? How he arranged the bodies?"

"Major probably told him," she said.

"True," said Reilly. "Look, you have to admit, he ticks all the boxes. He had a motive. He knew how to arrange the body. He wouldn't have any qualms about—"

"About murder? That's what you think of him?" she said. "Because he's not like that. He's not violent. He has nightmares..." Even as she was saying it, it all sounded flimsy.

"Okay," said Reilly. "Okay, I'll drop it. We'll look elsewhere."

"If Hawk had killed someone, I would know," she said. "I'm a profiler, Reilly. I would be able to *tell*."

"Sure." Reilly nodded vigorously. "Of course you would. I had to bring it up, but now that we've talked it out, it's fine.

We won't talk about it anymore."

"Okay," she said, going back to the window.

"Okay," he said.

* * *

"Oh, come in," said Alice Campbell, opening her door wide into her kitchen, where the smell of something baking was wafting out. "I'm so glad you came by. No one's been by to talk to me about Oliver, no one at all."

Reilly and Wren stepped into the kitchen.

Alice ran a rag over the round, wooden table in the corner. "Sit down, please."

Wren hesitated, and then sat.

Reilly sat down too.

Alice washed out the rag, wrung it out, and hung it over the faucet in the kitchen sink. Then she joined them. "Listen, this might sound a bit odd, Wren — er, Ms. Delacroix — but I wonder if you would mind staying a little after we talk. I have something I want to tell you."

Wren's mouth felt dry. So, then Oliver hadn't told his mother that he'd broken the news of his father to Wren? Of course he wouldn't have told his mother that he'd suffocated her and thrown her in a well. That was exactly the kind of thing you kept from your mom. Well, Wren guessed, anyway. With her own mother, it was a different story, she supposed.

"Would that be okay?" said Alice.

"Uh, yeah," said Wren. "Sure."

"Excellent." Alice smiled at them. "Um, how can I help you? Anything I can do to help, let me know."

"Well," said Reilly, "we're at square one with this, I'll be honest with you. We're working with several possible scenarios for why this happened to your son. In several of them, he's a target only because of he's his father's son. In others, however, he could have been a victim for personal reasons. Is there anyone you can think of who hated your son?"

"No," said Alice. "Really, no. I have thought this through, and I can't think of anyone. My daughter and I stayed up last night, just trying to put the pieces together, and we didn't get anywhere."

"So, he didn't have any enemies?" said Reilly.

"None," said Alice.

"Not at work? Not an ex? Not an old rival from high school?"

"Nothing like that," said Alice. "Oliver isn't currently employed. He's been staying home to help out his younger sister, Emmaline. She was diagnosed with leukemia, and she's needed care. I've been working, and Oliver volunteered to help Emmaline full time. So, there's no one at work. As for exes, there's only one that I'm aware of, from college. Oliver hasn't seen her in years, and she lives across the country. And he was very well-liked in high school. But I don't know. Maybe I'm not the person to ask."

"Who would be?" said Reilly.

"Possibly his best friend, Mack," said Alice. "Oh, his first name is really Alexander, but he goes by Mack. Mack Upton."

Reilly scribbled down the name. "Well, if you think of anything else, you'll give us a call, right?" He fished out a card and slid it across the table to her.

"Of course." Alice took the card and studied it.

Reilly got up from the table.

Wren got up too, hoping that Alice would somehow forget that she needed to talk to Wren to tell her about Adrian Campbell. She didn't know what to do. Should she lie about Oliver having told her about her father?

Yes, of course she should. There was no point in smearing a dead man's memory with what he'd done. Let it be. Oliver wasn't going to be contradicting her anytime soon. No one would ever know.

But Alice reached out for her. "Oh, Wren." She swallowed. "Ms. Delacroix."

"Right," said Wren, and sat back down.

Reilly shot her a questioning look.

She waved him out the door. Then she turned her attention to Alice.

"Listen, this might not be easy for you to hear," said Alice, "and it's certainly not something I like to dwell on, because it's all so very painful for me. But I feel that you need to know. And, frankly, I need your help. With Oliver gone and Adrian gone, all I have left is Emmaline, and I can't lose her." She licked her lips.

"Yeah," said Wren, her stomach twisting into knots. "That must be really hard."

Alice's eyes filled with tears. "You have no idea." She took a breath. "But I must say, one thing I have learned is that the human spirit is capable of handling things far worse than one might imagine it can. And when things get worse, you tend to find that you can handle it, if you must."

Wren only nodded. What should she say to that?

"I don't mean to shock you entirely," said Alice. "You have the last name Delacroix, so you have been brought up thinking that one man is your father—"

"I know Hayes Delacroix isn't my biological father," said Wren.

"Oh," said Alice. "Yes, well, so you're aware of that. That's good."

Wren swallowed. "I, uh, am aware that your late husband…" She let the sentence trail off. "That he was one of my mother's many affairs."

"You are?" said Alice. "Oh, well, then, perhaps this will be easier than I thought."

"You think it's possible that Adrian Campbell was my father, and that I might be a match for Emmaline for a transplant?" said Wren.

"Yes," said Alice. "How did you know?"

"I just put it together," said Wren. "Because of what you said about leukemia. It's bone marrow she needs?"

"Yes," said Alice.

"If I'm a match, of course I'll be a donor," said Wren.

Alice smiled, and tears spilled out of her eyes. "Thank you so much, Wren."

"Of course."

"I'm sorry that I never approached you before—"

"It's understandable why you wouldn't," said Wren. "It must all be very painful for you. I'm sorry, for whatever it's worth. I'm sorry about everything." And then she knew she had to get out of there, because she was beginning to feel like she might start crying too, and she knew that she couldn't do that. She shook Alice's hand, said her goodbyes, and fled.

***

"Hawk?" said Reilly, completely surprised to see the other man in his office. "You looking for Wren? Because she's off getting coffee." Reilly was pretty sure Wren just wanted some time to herself, actually, but he hadn't argued. She hadn't offered to get him anything from the Daily Bean, and he hadn't asked.

He figured that talking with Alice Campbell hadn't been easy for her, considering everything that had happened with Oliver.

But who *was* Oliver Campbell?

The kind of man who could do what he'd done to Wren, that kind of man had a darkness within him. He didn't buy that Oliver had no enemies at all. Of course, he still wasn't sold on the idea that the killing of Oliver had been personal. It was likely the work of a copycat serial killer. But if Wren didn't give him a profile to work with soon, he wasn't sure how they were going to look for that killer.

He didn't want to push Wren, though. Not now. Not after everything she'd gone through.

"No, I'm here to see you," said Hawk. "The other woman, Maliah? She told me to wait in here for you."

"Okay," said Reilly. "Well, what can I do for you?"

"I'm, um, just fishing around," said Hawk. "I don't know if this is even possible. I know that you used discretionary funds to hire Wren as an expert. I don't know, maybe you don't have any other funds, maybe they're all spoken for."

"You're asking for money?"

"I'm asking for a job," said Hawk. "Nothing permanent, just thought maybe you could use the help. I hear that there's another murder—"

"You hear that from Wren?"

"Well, I know she went out to see the body," said Hawk. "But, no, I haven't talked to her about it. She's been busy."

"So, you know who was killed?" said Reilly.

"No," said Hawk.

"Oliver Campbell," said Reilly.

Hawk gave him a sharp look. "You're kidding."

"Would I joke about this?"

Hawk folded his arms over his chest. "Well, that's very, very coincidental."

"Isn't it though." Reilly gave him a hard look.

Hawk straightened. "Oh." He nodded slowly. "Of course. I should have guessed that. No wonder she's avoiding me. She thinks I did it. You do too."

"Did you?"

"No."

The two men gazed at each other, and the words hung in the air.

"I had to ask," said Reilly.

"No, I get it," said Hawk. "I was angry with the man. He hurt Wren, and she wouldn't go through the proper channels to get justice…" He furrowed his brow, going very quiet suddenly.

"What?"

"Nothing," said Hawk. "I just, I had heard the murder was associated with the FCL, that there was more of the imagery that was present in the murders that Major committed. I thought maybe you might need some extra help with the cult angle. I thought maybe I could be of use in that way. That's all. But this is sounding... different."

"Why'd you trail off like that?" said Reilly.

"*Nothing.*" Hawk shifted on his feet, looking nervous. "Maybe I'd better go. This wasn't a good idea. After the thing with Baldwin, I was thinking maybe I wanted to get into law enforcement, and I thought this would be a good way to get my feet wet. But I didn't think it through. I'll just get out of your hair." He turned toward the door.

Reilly hurried around him and got between Hawk and the door. Reilly shut the door and stood in front of it. "I don't think so. Why'd you trail off? You were thinking about something."

Hawk's shoulders slumped. "It was an idiotic thought. I don't know why I thought it. Wren's not her mother. She doesn't care about vengeance. She would never..." He shook his head.

"Never what?"

"Really, let's drop this," said Hawk. "You going to move away from the door, Detective?"

"Vivian didn't kill people herself," said Reilly. "If she wanted vengeance, she got someone to carry it out for her."

"What's that supposed to mean? Now, you're not just accusing me, you're accusing Wren? Really?"

"I'm not accusing anyone," said Reilly. "You're the one who brought Wren up."

"Because you forced me to. I would never say anything to hurt her. I would never betray her."

Reilly swallowed. Betray her? That was an interesting choice of words, wasn't it? He stared Hawk down.

Hawk broke eye contact and looked at the floor.

Reilly moved away from the door.

"I can leave?" said Hawk.

"You can leave," said Reilly.

Hawk shuffled out of the office, looking pathetic and

beaten.

Reilly didn't buy it. He'd seen the man talk another man into turning a gun on himself. Just the kind of smooth-talking man who could convince Oliver Campbell to go for a walk in the woods.

Or convince ten-year-old girls to come have ice cream with him?

But no.

Major Hill had confessed to those crimes. That case was solved.

And this stuff about Wren that Hawk had brought up, that was bullshit. Hawk was manipulating him.

Manipulating him to take down Wren? No, that didn't make sense. Reilly had seen firsthand how worried Hawk had been about Wren. He truly would never do anything to hurt Wren, not knowingly. So... what did that mean?

Reilly thought of Wren's eagerly drinking in a dead body. The way she looked at a crime scene in delighted interest.

He felt queasy.

And then he got on the phone and scheduled a visit to the local jail to see Major Hill.

CHAPTER THREE

"What the hell?" Wren said. They were standing in Reilly's office the next day. "Why are we going to see Major?"

"I don't know, just dotting some I's. Crossing some T's."

"How does that help us do that?" she said.

"We have to talk to him," said Reilly. "If this isn't a copycat, we need to know that. It's possible that Major didn't commit any of the crimes—"

"He *confessed*."

"False confessions happen, Delacroix."

She clenched her hands into fists and released them.

"Look, why are you so against doing this?" he said.

"I'm not," she said.

He gave her a long, hard look. "Why didn't you want to press charges against Oliver?"

Her lips parted. "What is this, Reilly?"

"Just answer the question."

"Not because I wanted to kill him myself," she said. "I told you why. Come on. You saw what Chief Thomas was like. They hate me in Cardinal Falls. They'd never take it seriously. It wasn't worth it. It just wasn't."

He surveyed her.

She pulled out a chair in front of his desk and sank into it. "Okay, look, I probably would have eventually caved and pressed charges, because I couldn't have let him get away with it. But it would have been hell, and I wasn't ready yet."

He scratched his jaw.

"Come on, Reilly, if you really suspect me, suspend me from the case or something."

"I should anyway," said Reilly. "You have personal beef with Oliver. And he's your brother. And he's dead. It's all highly irregular for you to be investigating this."

"I know," she said. "I can sit it out if you want."

"No, I need you there when we're talking to Major," he said. "And this case involves the Fellowship. I need your expertise. I need you, Delacroix, so you're not sitting this out."

"Damn it," she said.

He cocked his head to one side. "We can stop for coffee on the way."

"We just got coffee."

"So? Can you have too much coffee?"

"Good point," she said, getting up.

"So, like, if it's a copycat, what's the profile look like?" said Reilly.

"Mmm, we need to know the places this crime scene diverges from the original crime scenes," she said.

"It doesn't," said Reilly. "Other than the fact that Adrian's not a little girl."

"He was drugged?"

"Same sedative given the girls. Not in ice cream, though. Looks like it was in a soda."

"And then suffocated?" she said.

"Yep."

"Exactly the same," she said, shaking her head.

"This is why we have to talk to Major."

"Right," she muttered. "Let's go."

* * *

"Wren!" said Major, when he was brought into the interview room where Reilly and Wren were waiting. It was a small room with a gray table in the middle and beige walls. Major tried to reach out for Wren, but the officer bringing him in stopped him. He cuffed Major to the table and told him to behave. Then, giving Reilly a salute, the officer left the room.

Major smiled a wide smile. "Wren, I'm so glad you're here."

"Well," said Wren, "it's not a social visit, I'm afraid. We want to talk to you about the girls you, um, saved from having to live out without their pairings."

"That's the thing," said Major. "I was confused before. I said that I killed those girls, but I didn't do it."

Wren felt the bottom go out of her stomach. "What do you mean?"

"Hawk did it," said Major. "It was always Hawk."

Wren swallowed hard.

Reilly leaned in. "Have you been hearing stories from outside the jail?"

"What?" said Major. "No."

"About other murders happening while you're locked up?"

"There are?" Major's eyes lit up. "Well, see, that proves it. It's not me. I knew Hawk wouldn't be able to stop. He said he would, but I knew he'd keep going, and—"

"You confessed," said Wren. "Why did you confess if you didn't do it?"

"Well, Hawk got me all mixed up." Major raised his shackled hands and twisted them up. "We'd do acid together, and he'd start talking. You ever listened to that voice of his? He's practically like a hypnotist."

"What?" said Wren. "No, he's not."

"You know who he's like?" Major pointed at Wren. "He's like your mom."

"Hawk is nothing like Vivian," said Wren, and there was something in her mouth that tasted bad and she wished she could spit or throw up or drink water.

"After he would do it, kill one of the girls, he would trip on acid with me, and he would tell me all the details. And I would start seeing what he said, and he would tell it like…

24

like I was there, you know? So, I would imagine it, see every moment of it. It started making me feel like I *did* do it. I had these images in my head, like memories. But I never did anything. Hawk did it. It was always Hawk."

"It couldn't have been Hawk," said Wren. "The night that Jenny Smith was set up, Hawk was with me. You remember, because you came and got him out of my bed. You were looking for him. You were upset."

Major just shrugged. "If you say so."

"You did come," said Wren. "You stood over my bed and scared the hell out of me."

"Did I?" Major looked confused.

Wren felt twin sensations rising in her. One, a horrible dread, the other, a raging fury. They twined around each other, batted against the back of her skull.

"Everything around that time is kind of a blur," said Major. "Sometimes, Hawk would make us do meth. When you do meth, you stay up for, like, four days straight, and you really start having weird hallucinations, and you can't tell reality from your dreams, because you're having them while you're awake... I think it was during one of those times that Hawk convinced me that I had a thing for you, Wren."

"What?" said Wren. "You don't?"

"No," said Major. "Now that I've been in jail and I'm totally clean, I'm not confused anymore. And I never liked you, not like that. I mean, you've always been nice, but... come on. Do you ever remember me even flirting with you?"

Wren twitched, because she was remembering a conversation with Hawk, where she'd asserted the same thing. Major had never shown any interest in her. But Hawk had insisted, and then later, Major had said...

"You're not confused anymore, because you want out of jail," said Wren. "When we arrested you, you were angry with Hawk. And I hear that he stopped coming to visit you recently. So, now you're probably even more angry. Angry enough to try to throw him under the bus to save yourself."

"That's not what I'm doing," said Major. "I swear, that's not what I'm doing."

Wren looked at Reilly. "I don't think we're going to get anything useful out of him."

Reilly nodded. "Okay." He got out of his seat and went over to rap on the door, signaling to the police officers out there that they were done.

"Wait," said Major. "You don't believe me? You have to believe me. I know that you and Hawk have this connection with each other, but you're not seeing him clearly. He's messing with your head. He's been doing it all along."

"Major, we didn't come here to get you out of jail," said Wren. "You killed those girls. You confessed. You knew all the details. It was you."

"It was Hawk," said Major.

CHAPTER FOUR

Reilly glanced at Wren, who was sitting completely still on the other side of his car. "You all right?"

"No," she said. "I'm not. How could I be okay?"

Reilly gazed out at the road. They were heading back to headquarters, but he wasn't in any rush. He took the curves slow. "He's smart, Wren."

"Who is?" She stared straight ahead.

"Major is," said Reilly. "He was smart enough to execute all those murders, hide the evidence, pose the bodies, everything. He's been locked up all alone with nothing to do but think. He's figured out all the angles. So, of course he could present something that sounded plausible."

"Hawk and I got in a fight at my dad's wedding."

" Yeah, I remember him saying something like that. Never did tell me what it was about, though."

"It was about the fact that I still suspected him," she said. "He got mad that I had ever thought that he was capable of killing little girls, and he got on a plane and came home early."

Reilly glanced at her. "What are you saying?"

"I don't know."

They were quiet.

The scenery outside streamed by. Reilly held onto the steering wheel. Wren tapped her fingers on top of her armrest.

" Did you know he came to me asking for a job?" said Reilly.

"What?" she said. "No. Are you kidding me? What kind of job?"

"Well, he said that he was thinking of getting into law enforcement, and that he thought he could be useful to the task force because he knew about the cult."

Wren wrapped her arms around herself and massaged her elbows. "That's the weirdest thing I've ever heard. I've never thought that Hawk had the least bit of interest in law enforcement."

"I wouldn't have pegged him for it either," said Reilly.

"Did you tell him no?"

"I think it ended up that he withdrew the idea." Reilly sighed. "I guess I can't help but suspect him too, okay?"

"No," said Wren. "No, that can't be. It's like you said. Major's smart. He's had time to make it sound good. Hawk didn't do this. He can't have been free all along, just toying with us. Toying with me. No way."

"You're probably right," said Reilly. "That's a lot to lay at his feet."

She didn't say anything for several moments. "Okay, but... we both suspect him, so what do we do with that?"

"Maybe you should, uh, take a break with him?" Reilly looked at her again. He tried to put it gently. "If you two are together—"

"We're *not*."

"You're something," said Reilly.

She sighed.

"You're sleeping with him," Reilly said, laying it out there. "Maybe you should stop doing that because you can't be objective—"

"Look, you don't get to judge me," she said. "Not when you're no better when it comes to stupid decisions about your own love life."

"I'm not judging you." He was offended.

"Yeah, you could have fooled me."

"What did I say that sounded like I was judging you?"

"I don't know. That I needed to stop screwing him."

"I never used that word."

She sighed.

More silence.

Reilly had to make a turn ahead. He put on his blinker. "Look, I didn't mean... I'm sorry. Okay? I'm sorry."

She turned on him. "I said, 'What can *we* do?' Not what can *I* do. So, instead of telling me how to run my personal life, why don't we focus on what the task force should do—"

"Anything we'd do otherwise," said Reilly. "Look for evidence."

"We'd try to eliminate him." She lifted her chin. "Well, he has an alibi."

"Yeah," said Reilly. "But if either of us believed that was airtight, we wouldn't be talking like this."

"How else can we eliminate him?"

Reilly didn't answer. He was thinking about it.

"Okay, well, I say we focus on other people instead right now," she said. "That guy that Oliver's mother told us about? His best friend Mack? Maybe he knows something."

"Yeah," said Reilly. "Yeah, sure."

* * *

Mack Upton looked back and forth between Reilly and Wren. He seemed a little nervous. "Am I in some kind of trouble?"

"Nothing like that," said Reilly. "We're just here to talk to you about Oliver Campbell. His mother said that the two of you were good friends."

Mack pushed open the door to his apartment and stood outside with Reilly and Wren next to his front door. There was a concrete walkway that stretched down in front of all the other apartment doors and covering over the walkway. He shut his door behind him. "Uh, look, I used to be good friends with Oliver Campbell, but he and I haven't spent time together in a long time. Oliver's been pretty busy with his sister. Plus, he's changed."

"What do you mean, changed?" said Wren.

Mack huddled into his sweatshirt as a chilly breeze fluttered past them. "Well, it started after his sister was diagnosed. He took it really hard. He hasn't had an easy life, losing his father young and all, and then having to live through those trials when he was growing up." He glanced at Wren and then away. "I mean, I guess you know about that, sort of, just from the other side."

"I was never brought to the trials," said Wren. "But, sure, I can see how that would be tough for him."

"So, how did that make him change?" asked Reilly.

"He just got really cynical about everything, and it made him… mean," said Mack. "He would say that nothing we did mattered, that we were screwed no matter what. So, he figured it didn't matter if he was an asshole. He started doing things to me that weren't cool. He took me out on a guys' night and took me to a strip club, which I didn't like, and then he refused to take me home. I had to get a cab back, and it wasn't cheap. Then he stole my bank card and racked up a bunch of charges. My wife put her foot down. She said I had to cut him out of my life."

"I guess she wasn't amused about the strip club?" said Reilly.

"Not in the least," said Mack. "And she was right. He wasn't being a good friend to me. He was hurting me. Using me. And when he stole money from me, it wasn't just me he was hurting. It was my wife and daughter, too. If it were just me, I would have stuck it out and taken it. He's going through hell. He needs a friend. But then he crossed the line. You don't take food out of my baby daughter's mouth and then expect that we're cool. We're not cool after that."

Reilly nodded. "I get it."

"So," said Wren, "you don't hang out with him anymore."

"No. Why are you guys asking me questions about him, anyway?" said Mack. "Is he the one in trouble?"

"You don't know?" said Wren.

"Know what?" said Mack.

"Um," said Reilly, swallowing, "I really hate to be the bearer of bad tidings, but Oliver… he was murdered."

"What?" said Mack. "What do you mean? That can't be." He shook his head. "My wife made me scrub him out of my life. I blocked him on my phone, unfriended him on social media. He tried to use his mother's phone to call me once and I blocked that too. I guess that's why no one could get through to tell me."

"I guess you don't watch the news," said Reilly.

"No, not really," said Mack. "I figure if it's worth knowing, it's on Facebook, right? But I missed the fact that Oliver was killed? This…" He bit down on his lower lip. "I never got to say goodbye to him," he murmured. "He died thinking I was angry with him." Mack looked down at his feet. "I'm sorry," he said in a thick voice. "You're going to have to excuse me." He dove back into his apartment before either of them could say anything.

They both stared at the door.

"Should we knock again?" said Wren.

"He's probably not going to be able to answer anymore questions right now," said Reilly.

Wren furrowed her brow. "You really think he would have been able to keep from seeing it on the news?"

"I guess. If he had seen it, then he'd be lying to us. Is that what you're saying, that he's lying to us? Why would he do that?"

"Maybe to get out of the conversation?" said Wren. "I don't know about you, Reilly, but taking food out of his baby daughter's mouth kind of sounds like motive to me."

Reilly considered. "You're not wrong."

* * *

"Hey," said Maliah, waving to Reilly across the parking lot.

He hurried to close the distance between them. "Sorry, I'

m late."

"You're not late," said Maliah. "None of the movies are going to start for another five minutes at least. Depending on what we want to see, anyway. We never decided that."

"Oh, yeah, well, that doesn't matter to me," said Reilly. "I'll watch anything."

"Anything?" Maliah grinned. "How about this one then?" She pointed at a poster.

"That screwball comedy? Really? You like that kind of thing?"

"Sure," said Maliah. "Who doesn't like comedy?"

"Well, I don't really like comedy," said Reilly. "I don't like how ridiculous it gets. It pulls me out of the story."

"Oh, okay, well, let's watch something else. What do you want to see?"

"Uh ... " Reilly stuck his hands in his pockets and surveyed the movie posters. "Well, I'm guessing you wouldn't be big on the action thriller."

"Not really," she said.

"Or the superhero movie?"

"No," she laughed. "I'm guessing you don't want to watch the romantic comedy either?"

"Uh..."

"Damn," she said. "Haven't we ever tried to watch a movie together?"

"You know, I don't know that we have," said Reilly, who was trying to think of what they did together besides screwing, and coming up with a big blank. Hell, they never even went out to dinner together, because they didn't want to be seen together in public. They'd spent all their time together sneaking around.

"And we haven't even talked about the kinds of things we like?"

"Never came up."

She laughed again. "Okay, fine." She pointed. "What about that one?"

"The haunted house thing? You like that?"

"Well, I'm not crazy about it," she said. "But I could watch it."

"Yeah, I guess I could watch that," he said. "I'd rather watch that than a comedy."

"And I'd rather watch that than superheroes."

"Well, then, there we go." He offered her his arm. "Come on then, I'll buy us tickets. Let's go on a real, honest-to-God date, Maliah."

She wrapped her fingers around his bicep and grinned up at him. "Let's."

* * *

The movie was awful.

Reilly hated it. He wasn't a big fan of horror, but it was better than comedy. He could tell that Maliah wasn't a big fan either. They bonded over their shared dislike of the movie on the way home. Once there, on her doorstep, they dithered there, talking about nothing, until she finally asked him in.

Then they sat in her living room and struggled for things to say, now that they'd dissected the awful movie to death.

Finally, he just went for it, climbed across the room, slid his hand under the back of her neck, and kissed her.

After that, everything seemed to go well. They were good at this part.

But later, when he was lying in her bed, and she was snug against him, her head resting on his chest, his fingers lazily tracing patterns on her hip, he wondered what a relationship would be like five years down the road when they didn't want to watch any of the same movies. He imagined Maliah watching TV in the living room and him sprawled out in another room, both of them spending each evening apart.

He knew that distance. It had already happened in his marriage to Janessa. True, they had avoided each other because of conflict, and maybe he was worrying over nothing. Maybe there was nothing to the idea of watching TV separately. Maybe he was making a thing of something that was meaningless. But he wondered if he wanted to set himself up for a life of loneliness and separation.

* * *

There was a soft knock at the door to Wren's cabin. She was staying on the compound of the Fellowship of the Children of the Lord, because of the charity of her friend Kimora, who said it wasn't a big deal, because no one was using the cabin, anyway.

Back in the late 90s and early 2000s, when the cult was expanding, these cabins had been put up quickly, all over the place, but after the murders, people cleared out left and right, leaving lots of them behind.

She knew who was at the door. Only one person ever came to her house.

Well, no, that wasn't true. There were two people. Hawk and Reilly. Reilly didn't knock gently. She wished it was Reilly, though. She'd rather deal with another body. Or, no. She wouldn't. Because that would mean this was definitely a serial killer, not something personal against Oliver Campbell.

She yanked the door open to the cabin. "You can't be here."

Hawk held up a six pack of beer like a peace offering.

"Seriously, Hawk, everything between us is weird right now."

"Why?" said Hawk. "What's changed? You've been avoiding me, that's all I know. I thought maybe you'd want to talk."

"No, I've been avoiding you because I don't want to talk."

"Well, maybe I want to talk."

"Too bad."

"I thought we agreed," he said. "If either of us needed something, we'd be there for each other."

"That is completely twisting what I said." She shook her

head. "I wanted there to be less pressure, not more."

"We need to talk about Oliver Campbell," he said.

"Do we?" she said. "Why?"

"Come on, little bird. Let me in. I don't want to do this on the porch. We need to have this conversation indoors."

"We don't need to have any conversation at all."

His voice dropped in pitch. "Did you do it?"

She backed away from the door letting go of it, completely shocked. "What?"

He took this opportunity to come inside. He shut the door behind him.

"I did not say you could come in."

He went past her into her kitchen, where he opened the refrigerator and slid the six pack in. Taking out two beers, he shut the fridge. "If you did it, just let me know. I can help you."

Her mouth gaping, she shook her head at him. She couldn't find words.

He set the beers on the counter and used his lighter to pop the tops off. Then he handed her a bottle.

She took it. "How can you ask me something like that? It's like you don't even know me."

He laughed. "Is that what it's like? Really? Well, how interesting."

She scoffed. "If this is some passive aggressive move so that I can see what it's like to feel accused—"

"I'm serious, little bird," he said, and he looked serious. Deadly serious. "You didn't want to press charges against him. You acted breezy about it. And then he ended up dead. You knew the original case inside and out, so I'm sure you could have set him up any way you wanted. Don't tell me that you're so high and mighty that you wouldn't seek vengeance. I know you better than that. And don't forget that it was my arms you crawled into after the last time you killed a man."

She sputtered. "That—that's not the same thing at all.

Come on, Hawk. You know I would never..." She swallowed hard. "I mean, okay, maybe I can kind of see how you might think that."

"But you didn't do it," said Hawk.

"No," she said.

"You can tell me if you did," said Hawk. "I would protect you. I would do whatever necessary to help you hide it, if you needed me. You don't have to hide anything from me."

"No, I'm not hiding anything," she said.

"Okay." He took a swig of his beer. "Okay. I believe you."

"Well, thank you." She glared at him. "I'm not going to bother asking if you did it."

"No?" he said. "Well, is that because you don't think I'm guilty or for some other reason?"

"It's because if you did do it, you'd lie. If you did do it, you've been lying to me all along."

"I didn't do it," he said, holding her gaze, looking deep into her eyes.

She gazed back for several long, long moments, but eventually, there was something too naked and penetrating about his eyes looking into hers, and she had to break contact. She took a drink of the beer he'd given her. "You, uh, you asked Reilly for a job?"

"Yeah, that was a stupid idea." He leaned against the counter, surveying his beer.

"Since when do you want to work in law enforcement?"

"I don't know," said Reilly. "I went out into the field with him, you know? We talked to people. I started to realize that I might have a little bit of talent for getting people to talk. I never thought anything that I learned from Vivian would be useful, but there it was. Like, maybe I could do something good for once."

"Well, if you want to do that, you don't need Reilly," she said. "You could join a police academy. But you would need to get your GED."

"I was planning on that," said Hawk, taking a drink of beer. "I just thought that maybe while I was getting it all squared away, maybe I could help you and Reilly out some more."

She chewed on her lip.

"Look," said Hawk. "I'm in love with you, little bird. You know I am. I also know you're not in love with me."

"Hawk—"

"And you're right not to be. You should have more than what I can offer you right now. To be the kind of man that you could love, I need to change. I just… I want to change. I really do."

She licked her lips. She watched him.

He looked up at her, and his eyes were vulnerable and gray and piercing.

She closed the distance between them, taking his beer bottle away, setting it on the counter. She ran her fingers over his neck and his shoulder and then dragged them down his chest. She kissed him.

CHAPTER FIVE

Reilly knocked on the door of what used to be his house, but was now Janessa's house. He didn't come here often, but Janessa had called and asked if he could come over one day after work. She said she had something to tell him, and she'd sounded excited.

He'd agreed warily. The last time Janessa had news, it was that she was pregnant and getting married to another man. Reilly still wasn't completely pleased about that development, but he'd managed to quell his crazy behavior over it. When she'd told him, at first, he'd been angry, and he'd set about trying to prove that she'd been having an affair while they were married. But then he discovered the reason for her getting married so quickly was that she was pregnant. Then he'd been angry about that too.

He realized now, though, that none of it had to do with Janessa.

Well, maybe he'd been helped to realize this by the shrink he'd had to go see. He'd been supposed to be talking to the shrink about how he was dealing with the fact that he'd shot Kyler Morris. But he hadn't shot Morris. Wren had done it. So, he hadn't had much to say about the act, and somehow the session had transitioned into talking about his divorce.

Anyway, he now realized that it all had to do with himself. He didn't want Janessa to get married and have another baby, because she got another chance to be happy. Reilly wanted that chance, too, but he was ashamed of himself for wanting it, for not having been satisfied with his family the way it was. He felt guilty for not loving Janessa enough, but he felt even guiltier because he wasn't sure he'd loved Timmy enough either.

The shrink said it was normal for parents to feel disappointed in their children. It happened all the time. That was why people were always dealing with disapproving parents. She said that there was no problem with his disappointment as long as he owned it and recognized it as his problem, not as his child's. As long as Reilly was aware that the shortcoming was his own, he was ahead of the game. Reilly could change himself, but trying to change his kid would be painful and next to impossible.

Anyway, Reilly was feeling very Zen about it all. So, he agreed to come by when Janessa asked him to.

She opened the door. "Caius, you're here."

"I'm here," he said, jamming his hands into his pockets.

"Come with me," she said, leading him into the living room, which looked so similar to when he used to live there as to be disturbing. When he moved out, his entire world changed. But for Janessa, only one thing changed. He wasn't there anymore.

He sat down on the couch he'd helped pick out, the one he'd paid for in three installment payments because they couldn't afford to buy it outright.

Timmy was sitting on the floor, building a track for his trains. He was babbling to himself as usual. Timmy was delayed in speech. He spoke, but he only repeated things that he had heard. He had very little spontaneous, meaningful language.

"Okay," said Janessa, sitting down next to him. She had a big paperback book in her arms and she thrust it at Reilly.

He took it and furrowed his brow. "*Obtaining Language Naturally on the Autism Spectrum*," he read. He turned to her sharply. "You've fought an autism diagnosis his whole life."

"I know," said Janessa. "Because I didn't want to give up

on him. I didn't want people to say, 'Oh, he's autistic,' and decide there was nothing else they could do. But even without the diagnosis, that's what we all did, Caius."

He opened his mouth to protest, but then he didn't. She was right, in way. They had all given up on Timmy in various ways. He still had a hard time accepting that this was all his son would ever be, but he didn't know how to reach him. Timmy didn't seem to want to be reached.

"You have to read the book," she said. "There's a boy in there, older than Timmy when he started the therapy, and he can talk now." Her eyes filled with tears. "I mean, he doesn't sound 'normal,' you know? It's not a miracle, but... we could communicate with him. We can, in fact. He's trying to talk to us, Caius. He's trying."

"What do you mean?" said Reilly, looking at her, and now his heart was starting to pick up speed.

"Do you ever notice how sometimes, when he does one of his quotes it seems..."

"Oddly appropriate?" said Reilly.

She nodded. "Yeah."

"Like, uh, one day I tried to give him a hug, and he pushed me away and said, 'The island of Sodor is surrounded by water on all sides.'"

Janessa brightened. "Exactly like that. He was trying to tell you that... that..."

"That he wanted to be an island," said Reilly. "He didn't want a hug. I *knew* it. I knew he was saying it, but I talked myself out of it."

Janessa touched her chest. "I've done that too. I thought that it was wishful thinking on my part, that I wanted him to be in there so badly that I was projecting."

"Me too," said Reilly, and now he was starting to feel excited. "Why didn't we ever talk about this before?"

"Oh, Caius, we haven't been very good at talking to each other in a long time."

He looked away. She was right. He licked his lips. "Okay,

so, uh, what's this book all about?"

"Well, it's a little hard to explain," she said. "But basically, the general thesis is that Timmy is a gestalt learner, meaning that he doesn't understand that language is made of smaller units that are put together. He's memorizing every single utterance he hears. He needs to learn to break them down, to see that they're made up of building blocks. Other kids, normal kids, they get that, but he doesn't. And he's not alone. There are other kids out there who are the same as him. There are stories in this book, case studies. I read them and bawled." Her eyes were shining.

"Really?" He turned the book over. "Okay, this seems cool. I'll look at it. So, what do we do? How do we help him break stuff down?"

"Um, the first step is just to repeat back to him what he's saying."

"That's it?"

"It's amazing, Caius. Try it, you'll see. He's spent years of his life thinking that nothing he says is important. No one ever responds to what he says. He has a few gestalts he can use, like 'yes,' or 'no,' but otherwise, we don't acknowledge anything he says."

"Right, because we don't think he's saying anything."

"When you start showing that you hear him, and that you're listening, he lights up." Tears started spill out of her eyes and she dashed them away. She pointed. "Try it."

Reilly hesitated. "Just repeat back what he's saying? Really?"

Janessa nodded.

Reilly took a deep breath and then he got down on the floor and crawled over to sit with Timmy. "Hey, Timmy."

Timmy looked up. "Hi. I'm Thomas," he chirped.

Reilly licked his lips. "Hi. I'm Thomas," he repeated.

Timmy grinned, a huge grin that Reilly had to admit he never saw on the kid. "I'm going to beep-beep at Percy." He lifted his chin. "Beep-beep!"

Reilly chuckled. "Beep-beep!"

"Beep-beep!" said Timmy again, delighted. He was making eye contact with his dad, and he was there. He was in there.

"Beep-beep!" said Reilly again, only his voice cracked.

"I'm going to beep-beep at Percy. Beep-beep!"

"I'm going to beep-beep at Timmy," said Reilly.

Timmy let out a peal of laughter, as if Reilly had just said the most amazing thing he'd ever heard. "Beep-beep at Timmy! Beep-beep at Timmy!"

Reilly laughed too, but his chest was tight. Timmy had repeated what he'd said back to him. That was immediate echolalia, something Timmy used to do, but had stopped a long time ago. Now, Reilly realized it was because he must have decided it was pointless, since no one had ever responded well to it. Reilly used to hate it, but now, hearing his son say back his words, he was overjoyed, because it meant Timmy was hearing him, that he was in this moment with Reilly.

For so long, he'd thought that his son was lost in another world, an impenetrable world. But all along, he'd been right there, waiting. Reilly, seized with emotion, wrapped his arms around Timmy.

Timmy squawked. "No! No! My doctor has forbidden me to push." He slithered out of Reilly's arm and hopped over to his trains, where he began to play with them on his own, making them talk to each other. He yammered out Thomas dialogue back and forth, but he looked up to see if Reilly was watching.

Reilly was.

"You see?" said Janessa softly, and she was on the floor next to him.

"Yeah," said Reilly.

Her eyes were red, and she had a tissue, wiping at her tears. Janessa raised her voice and repeated one of Timmy's lines back to him.

He beamed at her, pleased. He brought his trains over to his parents and showed off his toys. Reilly didn't think he'd ever done that before. He used to be so jealous of parents at parks, their children yelling, "Look at me, Daddy," because Timmy never seemed to care if he was looking at him.

Timmy cared.

Timmy was in there.

Reilly snatched a tissue out of Janessa's tissue box.

* * *

Wren looked up. Reilly was at the door to her office with his coffee cup. "Thanks for picking this up for me."

"Is it cold?" she said. "I thought you'd be in earlier."

"It's fine," he said. "I can pop it in the microwave if I need to."

She wrinkled up her nose. "That's coffee abuse."

He laughed. "Well, lukewarm coffee is an affront to all that's good in the universe, so I'll do what I have to do."

She eyed him. "You're in a good mood."

"Uh, I guess," said Reilly. "I found out some good news about my son yesterday."

"Oh, really?" Wren knew that Reilly's son was basically nonverbal, and that he was pretty torn up over it. "What happened?"

"Janessa found this therapy for echolalia," he said. "We don't know how far Timmy will be able to advance, but what's important is that he's actually trying to interact with his environment, he's not just stuck in his own little world. He just doesn't have the tools to understand how to form his own language, so we're going to try this thing to help him."

"Wow, that's cool," she said. "You think it'll work?"

"I don't know," said Reilly. "But the first step, it was pretty amazing. I don't know if I've ever seen him engage with anyone else like that before. Last night, for the first time in my life, I played with my son."

Wren grinned. "That's amazing."

"I mean, to anyone else, it wouldn't have looked like

playing, and he's still only repeating stuff, you know? But it was communication, like, two-way communication. You could tell he's been starving for it." Reilly looked away, his voice thick.

"So have you," said Wren.

He laughed. "Yeah, I guess so."

"So, how's it work?"

"I don't even know exactly. I have a book to read that Janessa got for me. But I guess that basically, we have to help him break down the things he's saying and realize they all have words in them and then put the words together himself. He's older, so he may be past the plasticity stage, he may never be able to talk completely normally, but he should be able to communicate more than just repetition. Janessa and I both think he can make progress."

"Oh, wow, Reilly, that's so great. I'm so happy for you." She smiled at him.

"Thanks," he said. "Uh, what are you doing in here so early?"

"I'm, um, trying to work on a copycat profile."

He arched his eyebrows. "I thought you were coming down pretty hard on the idea that Oliver's murder was isolated."

"Well, that's still a possibility. And it's also possible that Major didn't do it, that Hawk did. Or that someone else did all of it. Or that Major did it, and this is a copycat. We need to investigate all the possibilities."

"Okay," said Reilly. "I agree. So, how's your profile coming?"

"Well, it's tough to profile someone from a copycat crime scene, because whatever they've done is the work of a different mind. But there are two major theories about why people commit copycat crimes. One is that by taking on the identity of someone else, the killer is able to depersonalize. It's no longer him committing the crime, but instead it's another killer. This way, he's not bound by his own inhibitions. The other theory is that the killer craves the spotlight. If another killer has already had media attention, the killer might copy his crimes so that he can have that notoriety as well."

"Which do we think is more likely here?"

"Well, it really could be either," she said. "But we've got no indication that the killer is interested in fame here. If so, it seems like he might have left his own personal mark on the crime scene. But he copied exactly what Major did. So, that means it's likely the case of taking on a persona in order to have the ability to carry out the crime. Which means that we're probably looking for someone somewhat timid. He'd be shy, unassuming. He may still live with his mother or with an overbearing female replacement for the mother—"

"Why mother?"

"It's an infantilized relationship," she said.

"Okay," said Reilly. "Go ahead."

"He may have finished high school, but probably doesn't have a college education. He's probably unemployed or employed in a profession that shames him, like as a custodian or a garbage collector. He has an intense fantasy life. He probably is a massive fan of real serial killers, also of violent horror movies and graphic video games."

"All right," said Reilly. "Sounds good. Age range?"

"I'd say mid-twenties to late thirties," she said. "Old enough to have given up hope that life will get better, but not so old as to have given up entirely."

"This is all great stuff, Wren."

"Thanks," she said. "I've got the uniforms looking into the entertainment angle, asking local shops if they have anyone who fits the profile and buys a lot of movies or games. Unfortunately, we're probably not going to find him that way, because it's likely he doesn't shop locally. He probably just illegally torrents everything online."

"Maybe Maliah could look into that."

"Maybe," said Wren.

"I'll ask her," said Reilly.

* * *

"Well, it's theoretically possible to find out what people are torrenting," said Maliah. "Assuming they aren't cloaking it in some way, which is fairly easy to do. But without someone for me to target, I don't know what I can do."

"So, you need a specific target," he said.

"Yeah, I do," said Maliah.

"Okay," said Reilly. "Well, it was worth a try." He started out of her office.

"Hey," she said. "Aren't you going to tell me about your son?"

He turned back to her. "What? What do you know?"

She sighed. "Okay, I overheard a little of what you were saying to Delacroix. You told her, but not me?"

"I…" He spread his hands. "I was going to tell you. Of course I was going to tell you. I was going to tell you at dinner tonight. We're still on, right?"

"Yeah, we are," she said.

"Great," he said. He crossed the room and leaned down to kiss her. "See you later, then."

"Later," she said.

* * *

"Well, what do you think?" Maliah was cutting her steak. They were out at a nice restaurant in Shepherdstown, one that was pricier than what Reilly usually sprang for, but for some reason, he felt like he had something to prove. "Do you think it's a copycat?"

"It could be," said Reilly.

"You don't think it's that Hawk guy?"

"I don't know."

"But you've got to be leaning one way or the other," said Maliah.

"I…" He popped a shrimp into his mouth and chewed.

"Are you refusing to consider Hawk because of Delacroix?" said Maliah. "Because you can't do that, you know."

He swallowed his shrimp. "Hey, come on. Give me some credit here, Maliah. You think I'm the kind of guy who would do that?"

"You don't have to act all defensive," said Maliah, bringing a bite of steak to her mouth.

"I'm not defensive," he said. "Okay, maybe a little."

Maliah finished chewing. "Yeah, you're defensive because you're guilty. You're deliberately avoiding looking into him."

"I'm not doing that," said Reilly. "I don't even like the guy. If it's him, I will definitely arrest him."

"Even if it pisses off Delacroix?"

"Of course," said Reilly. "You think I'd let a murderer go free? Really? It's like you don't even know me."

"You are protesting way too much." She pointed at him with her fork.

"I am not!" Then he laughed. "No, I mean, I'm protesting. But I'm seriously not… I don't know where this jealousy thing comes from with you. Why do you think I'm into Wren?"

She looked down at her plate. "I'm not jealous."

"Since the moment you saw her, there's been tension."

"What? Since she showed up during our morning-after and you rushed down to talk to her?"

"Come *on*, Maliah."

She shrugged. "Well, it's not as though you haven't been unfaithful before."

Reilly's lips parted.

She ate more steak.

Reilly's voice was soft. "That's hardly fair. I mean, yes, I was unfaithful, but so were you. And it was with each other, so…"

"So, what? So, that proves that we have sterling characters?"

"No, it's only that I didn't cheat on Janessa because of

some defect I have. It's not a habitual thing with me."

"So, why'd you do it?"

"Why did you cheat on Jax?"

"He wouldn't have sex with me," she said. "We hadn't done it in four years. Not once in four years. I was going insane."

"Oh, maybe you said something about that once." He picked up his glass of wine and took a sip. "Sorry. I don't know why I forgot that."

"It's not something I liked to advertise," she said. "He made out like it was my fault. Like I didn't take care of myself, wasn't sexy enough..."

"That's bullshit," said Reilly.

"I know." She grinned at him. "I didn't know before. I believed him for a while, but then I saw you looking at me the way you looked at me, and I started to wake up and realize he was just being a dick."

"He was," said Reilly. "A total dick."

"And why was your infidelity a one-time thing again?"

He sighed. "Listen, Janessa and I just grew apart. We weren't having sex either, but neither of us were initiating. We just... fell apart. I don't know. We yelled at each other. We weren't good to each other. It was a toxic environment."

Maliah went back to her steak. "Well, it's all well and good to say this stuff, but the truth is that you and I were both presented with less-than-ideal relationships, and we chose infidelity to get through. There were other choices. Healthier choices. Choices that would cause others less pain. But we both chose to go down this path."

"What's your point?" he said. "Is your point that you're justified in being jealous of Wren?"

"I'm *not* jealous."

"Okay," he said in a tone that meant anything but okay.

"I didn't mean to pick a fight with you, Cai."

"Could have fooled me, because all you've done is insult me during this entire conversation."

"Now, that is not true."

"First, I'm such a crap police officer that I'm going to not properly investigate the case. Then I'm pandering to Wren. Then I'm probably going to sleep with Wren, since I'm a confirmed cheater—"

"You are twisting my words."

He sat back in his chair. He had lost his appetite. "Maybe we shouldn't talk about work."

She laughed. "Yes, definitely, Cai, this is all about work."

"You don't trust me," he said quietly.

"Do you trust me?" she said.

"Yeah," he said.

"Easy to say when you haven't been tested," she said.

"Let's talk about something else," he said. "Something less heavy."

"Okay," she said. "You're right." She speared one of her asparagus stalks with her fork. " What else do we talk about?"

"Um…" He tried to think, but the truth was that they hadn't engaged in a lot of conversations. Sure, they'd talked drunkenly at the bar, but that had been all about the subtext underneath, which was the maneuvering to get themselves into bed together. None of that had landed for him. He couldn't remember any of it.

"We do talk, don't we?" said Maliah, looking troubled.

"Yeah," said Reilly. "We talk."

But after that, they sat silently for a long time.

CHAPTER SIX

"So, it occurred to me that if we're putting Hawk back on the table, we should also put Isaac Scott back on the table," said Wren to Reilly. She was clutching the coffee he'd left for her on her desk and leaning against his office door.

"Is Hawk back on the table?" said Reilly.

"Sure," she said.

"If you say so," he said. "But, uh, who's Isaac Scott again?"

"He's an old guy who lives on the compound," she said. "He's still pretty devout. Follows all the teachings of the FCL. He's the one who found Jenny Smith's body."

"Oh, right, that guy." Reilly nodded. "Sure. I remember him. But didn't he have an alibi for one of the girls? He was at Virginia Beach or something."

"Right, well, I checked into that," said Wren, "and the uniforms were never able to follow up on it. They tried several times to contact the family that he was supposed to be on vacation with, but they couldn't get hold of them. Which doesn't mean that he was lying. But it does mean that he doesn't have an alibi."

"So, you're saying if Major didn't do it, Isaac could still be on the hook for everything?"

"Yes."

"Could he be the copycat?"

"I..." She shook her head. "Doesn't really fit the profile. Of course, there's always the chance that my profile is wrong. I don't entirely know how Vivian indoctrinated the

50

people that she got to murder for her. Maybe there are commonalities, enough to explain the similarities..."

"That's quite a leap," said Reilly. "None of the original murders carried out by the FCL bear any real similarity to Major's killings."

"I know," she said. "Pretty much everyone was shot, not drugged and suffocated. And they weren't arranged in the readiness pose. Something creepy like that would have pointed to the Fellowship right away. But maybe there's something more to it, something that's connected to her. A kind of symbolism."

"Well... what? Garrett Edwards and Lexi Hill, they're both in jail. And the other couple, the people who first turned Vivian in... what was their name?"

"Freeman," said Wren. "Karen and Terrence Freeman."

"They're the ones who disappeared, right?"

"They're dead," said Wren. "My mother must have had them killed, along with David Song. He disappeared too."

"You pretty sure about that?" said Reilly.

"Well, I don't have proof, but if you're asking if I think they showed up to kill Oliver Campbell, then no, I don't."

"Well, okay, then," said Reilly. "So, Isaac Scott."

* * *

Isaac Scott was carrying a shovel over his shoulder. He had been transplanting rose bushes out by the amphitheater. He was a bit of an all-around handyman for the FCL. "I'm not still a suspect, am I? I thought you arrested Major."

"We did," said Wren. "And we're convinced we got the right man. But in case we didn't, we just want to talk to you about the night when Oliver Campbell was murdered. Where were you?"

"Oh, Lord," said Isaac, setting down the shovel, the blade biting into the earth. "I can't even remember. It was a typical day. I could have been anywhere on the compound. The truth is that I spend a lot of time alone."

"Try to think," said Reilly. "It was a Monday. You do

anything specific on that day of the week?"

"No, I don't have a weekly routine. I just go where I'm needed," said Isaac. "I could ask Kimora. She might now. She has the schedule for me."

"I'll ask Kimora," said Wren. "Don't worry about that."

"But you insist on thinking that I did it," said Isaac. "Even though I thought I told you I was on vacation with the Daramonds."

"You did," said Wren. "We're looking into that."

"Still?" said Isaac. "That was a long time ago."

"I'm sorry," said Wren. "We're just having trouble getting in touch with the Daramonds. But what I'm going to do is go by and talk to them myself. I don't think they've taken well to phone calls from the police." She turned to Reilly. "Sometimes people on the compound don't much like outside interference."

"Yeah, we'll go there after this," said Reilly.

"Good," said Isaac. "And you'll see that I'm innocent. I would never have done such a thing."

"Listen, Isaac, I don't want you to take this the wrong way," said Wren. "But the thing is that you're very, um, devoted to the Fellowship. And I believe that you would do anything if you thought it was in the service of the Lord. Even killing."

"Well, that's not true," said Isaac.

"No?" said Wren.

"Didn't David Song say that if the word of your masters goes against the teaching of the Lord, you must deny it?"

"Did he?" said Wren. "I don't remember hearing David Song talk that much."

"Well, he did speak," said Isaac. "Much of the time. He did his best to guide his flock. But he himself was taken in by Vivian Delacroix. She was a powerful personality. He admired her. He was taken in by her fire. But he had no idea that she was doing such horrible things. If he'd known, he would have put a stop to it."

"Look, we don't know," said Wren. "Maybe David knew. Maybe he didn't. The fact that my mother killed him seems to lean towards the idea that—"

"She didn't kill him."

"Well, then where is he?"

"He's here with us," said Isaac. "As best as he can be."

"What, like spiritually?"

"Yes," said Isaac, picking up the shovel again. "Listen, is this going to take much longer—"

"So, you're telling me that if my mother had ordered you to kill someone—"

"She never did! I wasn't at those bonfires. I don't like to take too much LSD. I've done enough of that. It's a tool to expand one's mind, but my mind is plenty expanded, thank you very much."

"You were never there?"

"Never," said Isaac. "And if I had been ordered to kill, I would have refused, and I would have told her that she was working in the service of evil, and I would have kicked her out of the compound."

Wren raised her eyebrows. "Well, she wouldn't have listened to you. She might have had you killed."

"Right, well, I suppose would have gone to David Song, then," said Isaac. "Can I go now?"

* * *

Reilly pulled the car into the driveway of the Daramond cabin. "This the place?"

"Yeah," said Wren. "Looks right. I can't remember exactly, though. If it's not this one, it's the one next door. We'll try there if I got it wrong."

"All right," he said. "Hey, you really think Isaac Scott's our guy?"

"No," she said. "I don't."

"But we're going through a good bit of trouble to eliminate him."

"Might as well. Having someone good and eliminated,

it'll feel as though we've accomplished something."

"Or, we're just stalling," said Reilly.

Wren got out of the car and slammed the door.

He got out too. Why had he said that? He should keep his mouth shut. He followed her to the door of the cabin.

She knocked on the door.

A teenage girl answered the door, her hair in braids that hung down her back.

"Hi Vickie," said Wren.

"Hey," said Vickie. "I guess you want my mom."

"Actually, I can probably just ask you," said Wren.

"Ask me what? Don't you work with the police?" Vickie looked warily over Wren's shoulder at Reilly.

"I do, but you're not in any trouble, and neither is your family," said Wren. "I'm here to ask about Isaac Scott."

"What about him?"

"Last summer, when you went on vacation, did he come along?"

"Oh, yeah." Vickie made a face. "Yeah, he was there. It was so awkward. I can't believe my mother brought him with us. It was weird. He kept making all these comments about how vacations weren't really part of the Lord's plan for his children and stuff, but he was happy enough to eat our food and bask in the sunshine. He's kind of creepy, you know?"

"In what way?" said Wren.

"Well, my sister, Jessica, she's like eleven. I swear that old Isaac guy was checking her out in her bathing suit."

Wren turned to look at Reilly, who raised his eyebrows.

Then Wren turned back to Vickie. "But he was with you, at Virginia Beach? He was there?"

"Yeah, he was there. I just said he was, didn't I?"

* * *

"Well, he's got a confirmed alibi," said Wren from the passenger seat of Reilly's car. "We eliminate him. It doesn't matter if he was looking at girls in bathing suits. None of

54

that matters."

"Except it's bothering you," said Reilly.

Wren didn't say anything. Instead, she pointed through the windshield. "Take your next right."

"Got it," said Reilly, executing the turn. "It's bothering me, too, I can't deny it. Could he have been involved somehow? Could Major have had an accomplice?"

"Two of them," said Wren. "Right. I thought of that for the last case, but I never thought of it for this one. The crime scenes don't support it. They're focused and straightforward, an execution of one man's vision."

"Right," said Reilly. "Except that man with the vision is in jail, and we have a nearly identical scene."

"I know." She sighed. "Um, that cabin there."

"That one? With the tricycle in the yard?"

"Yup, that's it."

Reilly pulled up to park along the side of the road. "What if he's the copycat?"

"Except the copycat *didn't* kill young girls." Wren pointed at the cabin. "Anyway, maybe Kimora will know if there's a reason to suspect that he did it or not."

"Okay," said Reilly.

Wren opened her door, and Reilly followed suit. They got out of the car and walked over the gravel driveway to the walkway to the porch. They climbed the steps onto the porch, which was littered with Barbies, plastic toy shopping carts, and trucks. Wren knocked on the door.

The door opened and Kimora was there, baby on her hip. "Wren! Hey, long time."

"Hey," said Wren. "You got a minute?"

"I never have a minute," said Kimora. "I am busy all the time." Kimora headed up the historic preservation society that ran the tours of the murder sites. She also managed the upkeep of the public spaces on the compound. She had a lot on her plate, not to mention her three small children, which were always underfoot while she was doing scheduling and working. "But come in anyway."

Wren gestured. "This is Detective Reilly. I work with him."

"Oh, Lord," said Kimora. "Is this about the murder stuff?"

"Yeah," said Wren. "Basically, we know that you make a schedule for Isaac Scott, and we were wondering if we could try to figure out what he was doing the night that Oliver Campbell died."

"Um... yeah," said Kimora. She put her baby down in a bouncy harness that was attached to the door frame. Then she got out her phone and started scrolling on the screen. "What day was that again?"

Reilly told her.

"Oh, right," said Kimora. "That was the day that he went out to Hagerstown to pick up some stuff that we needed from Ollie's. They have a better selection and better prices than Wal-mart, so I send him there. But his truck broke down, and I ended up paying for him to stay at a hotel while he got it fixed, because I couldn't get anyone to go out there and get him. I couldn't go because of the kids, and everyone else was busy with tours and things. The tours have gotten so busy lately, what with Major getting arrested and stuff. I had to hire two new workers, even."

"Wow," said Wren. "That's good?"

"Yeah, it's amazing," said Kimora. "Anyway, is that a help to you guys?"

"Definitely," said Wren.

* * *

"So, stuck in a hotel in Hagerstown that night," said Wren.

"It's possible he left," said Reilly. "He could have gotten an Uber or rented a car."

"An Uber from Hagerstown to Cardinal Falls? That sounds pricey."

"True," said Reilly. "It's not probable, maybe, but it's

possible."

"Look, we wanted him eliminated," said Wren. "He's eliminated. Good. Let's move on."

"That's really how you feel about this?"

"It doesn't matter how I feel," said Wren. "The evidence points toward his not being involved. So, let's put him on the back burner for now."

"All right," said Reilly. "Except we've got no one on the front burner."

"I know," said Wren. "We'll figure it out, though. We will."

"You want to stop for coffee on the way back to headquarters?"

She grinned at him. "You know me so well."

He chuckled. "Let's get some caffeine."

CHAPTER SEVEN

That afternoon, Reilly left work early so that he could get to Janessa's house. Now that he and Timmy could have conversations, after a fashion, being around the little guy had taken on an excitement that he'd never quite known before. He was seized by the desire to get to know his little son, and he wanted to do it all the time.

Janessa had been very understanding. When he'd asked to come by and take Timmy out for dinner, she had said it was fine.

He hadn't been expecting that response. Truthfully, she never wanted to give Reilly extra time with Timmy, not unless she wanted something, and Reilly felt strongly that it was more about punishing him for diving into his work and abandoning his family than it was about anything else. The thing was, maybe he deserved it, but Timmy didn't.

This time, though, Janessa had been very accommodating. Then they'd chatted on the phone about the book she'd given him, and she'd asked him whether she should talk to his speech therapist about it, and he'd said that of course she should.

She was nervous. Didn't want to appear as though she was telling the woman how to do her job. Reilly said he'd go with her, and they'd get the woman to see that this was the best form of therapy for Timmy. He was confident the speech therapist would find it as exciting as they had.

He arrived at Janessa's place, and—for the first time—he didn't think of it as his old house. It was Janessa's. He didn't

live here. He knocked on the door and no one answered.
He waited.
He knocked again.
A call from within, far away. "Come in, Caius!"
He tried the door. It opened. He stepped inside. Now inside the house, he could hear Timmy wailing in the background.
Shit.
He left the living room and went up the steps to the upper levels of the house. He stopped in the doorway to Timmy's bedroom.
"Thomas goes to Tidmouth Sheds!" Timmy was sobbing. "Percy goes to Tidmouth Sheds. Thomas is a really useful engine." He was in the middle of the bedroom floor and he had taken off all his clothes except his underwear.
Janessa was kneeling in front of him, holding out his shirt. "Come on, babykins, let's put on your shirt. You want to go for pizza with Daddy, right?"
"No!" said Timmy.
"Hey," said Reilly from the doorway.
Janessa looked up at him. "Hey. I'm sorry."
"What?" he said. "It's not your fault." He knelt down next to her. "Hey, Timmy-Tim. It's Daddy."
Timmy looked at him and sniffled. He started singing the Thomas theme song in a wavery voice.
"Timmy," said Reilly. "We're going to go get pizza. That would be fun, right? You can bring your trains. We can play with trains at the pizza place."
"No," said Timmy, breaking off the song.
"Sure you do, babykins," said Janessa. "You want to go with Daddy. You love pizza. You love your Daddy. You'll have so much fun."
"Thomas, he's the cheeky one," sang Timmy. "James is vain, but lots of fun."
Janessa shut her eyes. "I think it's my fault."
"Janessa, nobody's blaming anyone," said Reilly, who

was coming to terms with the fact that he wasn't going to take Timmy to get pizza.

Janessa got up and went to the door.

Reilly followed her.

They stood in the hallway, outside Timmy's room, and the little boy continued to sing to himself.

"I didn't prepare him enough," she said. "I meant to. I really did. But my morning sickness has been getting worse, and then when I felt better, I wanted to play with him, and... the day just got away from me. I think I only told him about your coming once."

"Oh," said Reilly. "You didn't tell him what to expect."

"Yeah," she said. "I'm sorry. I really didn't do it on purpose, Caius. I swear. I actually have plans. I was going to go out with Garth tonight. I want you to take him." She rubbed her forehead.

"Hey, I believe you," said Reilly. "He's doing the end of the Thomas episode. That's the song. It's at the end of every episode, and this is the end of his day. He's trying to tell us that he doesn't like the change in his routine. He wants to have the normal end of his day, not something new and different."

"Oh, I think you're right." They both turned and looked at Timmy and Reilly could feel that even though they were frustrated, they were excited as well, because Timmy was communicating, and it was huge.

Reilly knew that if you wanted to change Timmy's routine, you needed to telegraph it. You needed to tell him five or ten times that things would be different, go through every permutation of what was going to happen, and make sure he knew what to expect. Otherwise, he would throw a tantrum.

In the past, he might have faulted Janessa for what she'd done. She knew as well as he did what was necessary to prep Timmy for a change in routine. But he didn't fault her.

"I don't think he's going to go with you," said Janessa. "I

can't get him dressed."

"Hey, it's okay," said Reilly. "He's too upset at this point."

"But I wanted—"

"When were you supposed to meet Garth?"

"Uh... in about twenty minutes."

"Well, how about you go and do that, and I stay here and give Timmy his typical dinner and a bath and put him to bed. I mean, he might still be annoyed with it being me and not you, but I do put him to bed when he stays with me, so it'll be better than trying to get him in a car. And then, your night isn't ruined."

"You would do that?" she said.

"Hey, I just wanted to hang with him. I don't care about pizza," he said, grinning.

She grinned back. "Thank you, Caius."

"Yeah, no problem."

She looked at him for a minute, her brow furrowing.

"What?"

"It's only... it's so easy to talk to you lately. It makes me wonder..." She twisted her hands together. "If we would have got him diagnosed when he was younger, maybe we would have found this therapy earlier. Maybe if I hadn't been so stubborn, we would have had hope for Timmy, and then we wouldn't have started hating each other."

"Hey, hey," he said. "There's no point in playing that game. I'm the one who destroyed everything anyway. I gave up. I ducked out. I disappeared in work, and I betrayed our vows. I exploded the marriage, not you."

She just gazed at him, surprise in her eyes, and he wondered if he'd ever taken responsibility out loud to her before. She'd certainly never said anything like what she'd said to him. "Cai... we can't go back."

"No, we can't," he said.

Her hand strayed to her belly, and she looked back at Timmy. "What you said before, about having another baby, a do-over—"

"I was out of line."

" Maybe it was true. I didn't have to put so much pressure on Timmy to be what I wanted him to be. I could let him be autistic if he was autistic. You know?"

"Don't beat yourself up, Jannie. You're a great mom."

She smiled at him.

Reilly inclined his head at Timmy. "I'll deal with him. You go get ready to leave and then you can say goodbye to him."

"Okay," she said. "Thanks again."

"Of course," he said.

* * *

" So, anyway," Reilly was saying to Maliah from the doorway to her office, "then, I go and open the refrigerator, and I get out the milk and juice. And I hold them up, and I say what they are. And I say, 'Which one?'" It was morning. Reilly had been by the coffee shop, but Angela had told him Wren had already been in to get his coffee, so he hadn't purchased anything.

"Okay," said Maliah. "I thought you told me that you stopped asking him to choose between stuff because he just repeated the last one you said, no matter what."

"No, you're right," said Reilly. "I mean, as I was doing it, I was thinking he was probably going to get mad and knock the milk carton out of my hand and I'd be cleaning up a spill. Because that's what he'd usually do. He'd say the last thing you said, and then you'd give him that, and it wouldn't be what he wanted, and he'd throw a fit."

"But I guess that didn't happen this time?"

"No," said Reilly. " No, he just looks at me, and I go, 'Timmy wants to drink…' And he says, 'Juice.'" A huge grin burst across his face. "He seriously said it. And he pointed. Like, he knew what we were talking about. He was right with me. It was crazy."

Maliah grinned back. "That's so cool, Cai. I'm so excited

for you. You know, sometime, I have to meet Timmy."

"Yeah, you do," said Reilly. "Uh, we should definitely—"

Wren appeared in the doorway, holding out a coffee cup. "I thought I heard you."

"Oh, great," said Reilly, taking the coffee away from her. "Thank you for this."

Wren gave Maliah a little wave. "Morning."

"Morning," said Maliah.

Reilly leaned over and kissed Maliah's cheek. "Talk later, huh?"

"Sure," said Maliah, who beamed up at him as if the kiss had made her morning.

Reilly smiled at her. Things were good for him. If this case they were working wasn't so damned confusing, everything in his life would be pretty perfect. He ambled out of the office, sipping on his coffee. " Hey, Wren, I got something to talk to you about."

She fell into step with him. "Okay. What?"

"Well, I got some communication from, uh, from Vivian Delacroix's lawyer."

Wren stopped walking at the mention of her mother's name.

Reilly stopped too.

" What's she want? " said Wren. " Is she trying to negotiate something?"

"She didn't say that," said Reilly. "The message I got was that she wanted to help. She thinks she has insight into our case."

" Which case? The copycat case? Does she even know about that?"

Reilly spread his hands. "I don't know. But I think we have to go and hear her out."

" Are you kidding me? That's a terrible idea." Wren started walking again.

He went after her. "Maybe so, but if we don't check into

this, we could be missing out on important information."

"She's lying. She doesn't know anything."

" That could be true, but we can't be sure. I know it would be tough for you to see her—"

"I'm not going to see her," said Wren. "Neither of us are. That's a stupid, bullshit idea." She turned her back on him. She walked stiffly down the hallway and into her office. Her door closed.

CHAPTER EIGHT

Reilly gently rapped on the door of Wren's office about ten minutes later. He had given her a little space to calm down, hoping she'd come out on her own, but she hadn't.

The door was yanked open and Wren stood there, her face twisted in fury. "When I was about six years old, I kept trying to climb up on the counter in our cabin, because it looked fun. I wanted to sit there and swing my legs over the side. And my mother told me to stop it. She said it wasn't safe up there. I wouldn't listen. The third time I climbed up there, she grabbed my hand and stuck it on the side of the toaster, which was right next to where I was sitting, and which had been recently used to make toast. It was hot. It wasn't like, third-degree-burn hot, but it hurt, and I screamed, and she wouldn't take my hand away, and she looked into my eyes and told me that it wasn't safe, and that I needed to know what pain was to be frightened of it, and that pain was nature's way of showing us our limitations, and that if I got badly hurt, people would think she was a bad mother."

Reilly licked his lips. "Listen, Wren—"

"I didn't get a blister or a bad burn from it. But it hurt, and it was red for days, and I cried and cried. When she was talking to me, when she had her face in mine, when she was explaining how my getting damaged would be a problem for her stupid reputation, I feel like that was when I really got to understand that woman. I don't talk to her anymore."

Reilly hung his head.

"She doesn't know anything," said Wren. "She wants something. She's never done a thing to 'help' anyone in her life, not without strings, and she certainly isn't going to help our case. She's playing us."

"All right, okay," said Reilly. "But we'll know that going in, so whatever she tries to say, we'll be on our guard, and if she doesn't give us any information, we won't play games with her. We'll leave."

"I'm not going to see her."

He sighed. "Okay." He nodded. "Okay."

"Good, let's drop this."

"What if I went and talked to Vivian on my own?"

"She would chew you up and spit you out," said Wren.

"Listen, I'm sorry that—"

Wren slammed the door in his face.

He sighed again.

* * *

Wren fought her way through the woods. These woods were owned by the Fellowship, and the last time she'd been out here, she'd been on her own, looking for Major, trying to save Hawk's life.

She had been frightened. She remembered that. She remembered the strange thoughts she'd had of the Crimson Ram. Those thoughts seemed to come back to her at the worst moments. When she'd had to leave the Academy, they had been triggered by the phone calls from David Song. Well, he hadn't been David Song.

Come to think of it, they'd never gotten to the bottom of those calls.

They'd solved the case, but there were still threads hanging, threads that needed tying off.

Like coming out into the woods here. Why hadn't someone done this already? Wasn't it the obvious thing to do? But she hadn't even thought of it, and it made her wonder if she was really seeing all of this rationally.

She had protested when Reilly had accused her of killing

Oliver, because she knew she was innocent.

Except now... the memory of the vivid visuals of the Crimson Ram, on a horse in a blackened forest, the stars raining down... What had been done to her all those years ago? When she came back to this place, she had done it because she was drawn to the bodies of those dead girls. Something about the death called to some part of her, some awful, dark part.

And she still remembered the way she'd felt after she'd shot Kyler Morris, the jolt of pure power that had lit her up.

She knew what all this stuff added up to, and it added up to her not being able to trust herself.

She looked along the path, and the thoughts formed unbidden in her brain. *Have I come down this path again? Did I come down this path with a body on a litter, dragging it behind me?*

No, no, no.

The logistics of it didn't make any sense. She couldn't have killed Oliver and then transported him all the way out here.

He was walking next to me, responded her brain, and she flashed on an image of Oliver walking next to her through the forest.

"Stop," she said aloud. It didn't mean anything. She'd told herself before that conjuring an image was nothing. Anyone would do it if it was described vividly enough. That wasn't a memory, it was her goddamned imagination.

But, whispered a scaly voice in her head, *wouldn't it have been easy enough to convince Oliver to come with you if you offered him help with his sister? Wouldn't he have done anything for her? Hadn't he already proved that?*

She was not going to think this. She tamped down her thoughts and she forced herself to make her mind blank. She wasn't going to think about anything.

She walked in silence, and there was nothing but the autumn leaves on the trees, occasionally falling to the ground here and there.

Then, there it was. The path that Major had taken. She turned onto it, and immediately came to the clearing, where the stone circle was laid out. It had been covered in piles of bones before, but those had all been collected for evidence.

She noticed that there was a new one here, a small pile of bones, like from a tiny animal—maybe a squirrel or a rat.

Giving the stone circle a wide berth, she walked out to where they had found the girls' clothes. It should be empty too, but it wasn't. There were clothes there. Men's clothes. Oliver's clothes. Folded neat and pretty as you please.

She turned away, pressing her palm to her forehead. "Why?"

She knew, though. If a killer were compulsive about his routine, he would be nearly powerless to change it. He would have to follow it, even if—

"But Oliver doesn't fit the victim's profile!" she shouted at the night sky.

Right, right. So, that meant that someone was trying to make it look like the same killer, but someone with such intimate knowledge of the crime scene that they would be able to recreate all this detail.

"Someone like me," she rasped.

I didn't do this and forget about it, she insisted. *I'm not crazy.*

She got out her phone and dialed. She held it to her ear. "Reilly?" she said when he answered. "We need to get a team out in the woods. There's evidence for Oliver's case."

CHAPTER NINE

"Why'd you come out here on your own?" said Reilly. They were outside the woods. The stars were bright overhead and the air was cool.

"I don't know," she said. "I should have had you come with me. But I didn't touch anything."

The team that Reilly had called in, assembled of the uniforms assigned to the task force this week, were still out in the woods, bagging anything they thought might be evidence.

Reilly licked his lips. "Yeah, well, Wren, it's not good. Now, you were out there, so if we find anything linking to you, we'll eliminate it, but... well, someone could say that you did that on purpose. That you came out here in order to have evidence of you eliminated. You needed to let me know about this. You're too close—"

"I'm *sorry*." She raked her fingers through her hair. "I'm sorry, Reilly. I shouldn't have come alone. I should have talked to you."

"You definitely should have."

She swallowed. "You think it's me."

"No." He shook his head, dismissing this, and she believed him. "I don't. I would never think that about you."

"Why not?" she said. "Because maybe someone should, you know?"

He gave her a long, long look. "Are you trying to confess something to me, Wren?"

"No. If I did it, I don't remember. If I did it, it was in

some kind of fugue state—"

"That's a real thing?"

"Sure."

"I don't think that's a real thing."

"I think it could be a real thing."

"I think that's a thing people say that happened, because they can't face what they really are."

"Reilly, I think I could have gotten him to come with me. I think I could have convinced him to walk out into the woods with me. If I promised him help with his sister, he would have done what I asked. I could have laid him out just like Major laid out the girls." She paused. "Of course, then I would have had to transport him out to where we found him. How would I have done that? I don't know if I could drag him. I mean, I'm not a weakling, but—"

"Stop it, Wren." He took her by the shoulders. "You have to pull yourself together. You would know if you did this. You didn't."

She didn't say anything.

"Look, I'm not sure if it's a good idea for you to stay on this case. Considering how close you are to everything, once we find the killer and arrest him, the guy's lawyer is going to use this to poke holes in whatever case we make. Besides, I feel as though you could maybe use a break."

She raised her gaze to meet his. "I think we should go see Vivian."

"What?"

"You're right. It's a lead. We need to follow up on any and all leads. Maybe she *does* know something."

He folded his arms over his chest.

She drew in a breath through her nose, nodding. "Yeah, that's what we should do. Make that happen, Reilly. Get us in to see her." She turned to watch as uniformed officers trudged out towards the road, where their cars were parked. She gestured. "I should maybe get home."

"Wren, I'm serious about your backing off the case."

"You'll need me if you want to talk to Vivian," said Wren, shooting him a glance. Then she gave him a half-wave and started after the other officers, leaving Reilly there, in the darkness.

* * *

When Wren got home, Hawk was sitting on her porch, a bottle of whiskey between his thighs.

"Go home," she said to him. She opened the door and went inside the house. Then she shut the door behind her. She tossed her keys on the table next to the door. She shrugged out of her leather jacket.

Behind her, the door opened.

She turned.

Hawk held out the bottle of whiskey to her.

She took it and took a big gulp. Then she grimaced as it burned its path down her throat. She gave it back to him. "I mean it. Go."

"Listen, Wren, where you been?"

"I went for a walk in the woods, out where Major killed those girls," she said, and she looked him straight in the eye. She wasn't sure what she expected him to do. Flinch?

He gazed back at her steadily. "Why would you do a thing like that?"

"Oliver's clothes were out there," she said.

"How'd you know that?" he said.

"Because I saw them," she said.

"You knew they'd be there before you went on the walk," he said. "You knew that because..." He took a drink of whiskey. "Did you put them there, Wren?"

"Don't do that." She pointed at him. "Stop doing that."

"Doing what?"

"I think you should go, Hawk. This is the third time I've said that."

He offered her the whiskey again.

She waved it away.

He didn't leave.

She hugged herself. "What happened? The night after I climbed out of that well, you were sorry. You seemed ... regretful. But you don't anymore."

"Don't I?" He hung his head, chuckling to himself. "Well, I guess I wonder, little bird, between the two of us, which of us is worse?"

Her jaw twitched.

He looked up at her. "I thought that you made me better, but then I realized that wasn't true. Whatever it was, it got too far in me. No one can get it out of me, not even you. Maybe especially not you. Maybe because it's also in you."

"What the fuck are you talking about?"

"The darkness, little bird. It's why you want me. Your darkness wants my darkness. It's what makes you pant and sigh and scream my name. It's what brings you to your brink over and over again. It's the part of you—"

"Stop." She whispered it.

But he listened to the whisper. He drank more whiskey and he wouldn't look at her.

"Go," she said hoarsely, pointing to the door.

He closed the distance between them, reached up and feathered his fingers over her cheekbone. "You sure that's what you want?"

Her lips parted, and she looked at him, at his penetrating gray eyes and his intense expression, and she thought of leaning close to him, putting her mouth on his skin, pushing aside his clothes, taking him back to her bed. She thought of how easy that would be, how it would even feel good, how it would be comforting. She wanted comfort and closeness and warmth right now. "Yes," she murmured. "Get out of my house. Now."

He did flinch now, as if she'd cut him. "Whatever you say, little bird." And then he hunched over and slunk out of the house, like a scolded dog.

CHAPTER TEN

Ms. Givens, Timmy's speech teacher, paged idly through the book they'd handed to her. "Huh, all very interesting," she said, giving them both an encouraging smile.

Reilly smiled back. "Well, we just wanted to let you know that we've been implementing it, and it's caused a huge breakthrough for Timmy."

"I actually am familiar with this." Ms. Givens closed the book and set it on the table in front of her. The table was small, kid-sized, which meant that it looked a little ridiculous next to their adult-sized chairs. The table was between Ms. Givens and Reilly and Janessa. "We did talk about it in my program at college. It doesn't have any clinical experimentation to back it up, however, so it's just the opinions of the person who wrote the book. In order to be recognized by the community, there has to be more work done."

"But the book is full of case studies," said Janessa.

"The book is full of anecdotes," said Ms. Givens.

Janessa gave Reilly a despairing look. Everything she feared was coming true.

Reilly felt a surge of his old protectiveness toward Janessa. Before she was typically upset at him, he used to hate it when she got upset. He'd do anything in his power to make her feel better. "Now, wait a second. We both read the book, and we started doing something so simple—just repeating back to Timmy what it was that he was saying—and suddenly, after years of nothing, we're making progress."

Ms. Givens nodded. "True. I've seen it. He's much more interactive. It's really amazing."

"So?" said Janessa. "You're just discounting the book out of hand even though you've seen what it's done?"

"I'm not," said Ms. Givens. "Really, I'm not. It's clear that whatever you've done, it's working, and I wouldn't discourage you from continuing it. I don't think the book is harmful, I'm just not sure if all the claims in it are based on sound science."

"So, what do you mean by that?" said Reilly, folding his arms over his chest.

"Well, I guess it could be possible that the method in the book does help create progress, but perhaps not for the reasons that the author thinks it does. This gestalt idea is seductive, but I'm not sure it's always borne out in testing among children. Whatever the case, the fact that you've both been interacting with Timmy, whether it's just repeating what he's saying or not, it's shown him that what he has to say is meaningful and that language can help him connect with other people, and he's made a decision to use language more and more to communicate."

"I don't think that at all," said Reilly. "He was always trying to communicate, but we weren't trying to understand."

Ms. Givens spread her hands. "That could be true. We don't know if Timmy was simply uninterested in the world around him before or if he was just unable to express himself."

"Of course he was interested!" said Janessa. "Why would you say such a thing?"

"For what it's worth, I think you're right," said Ms. Givens. "But the professionals who study this find evidence that supports the other point of view as well. Anyway, as I said, I think that the two of you should continue to do whatever it is that you're doing with Timmy. Keep up the good work, really. But if you're here to ask me to deviate from the state-appointed curriculum, I'm afraid I can't do that. It's simply not up to me."

Janessa sighed. "Oh, fine. Look, I'm not trying to tell you how to do your job, but I'm just saying, that this is insight into my son, who you work with, and I want you to have it."

"I'm grateful, really," said Ms. Givens. "I am. And I thank you both for coming down, and for being such great parents to Timmy. You're both so committed and caring. I can tell that. He's a lucky little boy."

Reilly could tell she was tying up the conversation, wanting it to be over. "We really weren't intending any offense," he said.

"And none's taken," said Ms. Givens. "I hope I haven't offended you. I'll be Timmy's speech therapist while he's at this school, so we still have some time yet to work together, and I want our relationship to be a good one." She smiled widely.

"Sure," said Janessa. "Of course."

The meeting was basically over after that. They talked a little longer, but not about anything of consequence, and then they said their goodbyes and left.

Reilly and Janessa walked out of the building together. Outside, they paused in the parking lot before getting into their respective cars.

"I feel like we just wasted our time," said Janessa.

"Yeah, it didn't go as well as I'd hoped," said Reilly.

"I'm glad you came, anyway," said Janessa. "It means a lot. Thank you so much."

"Sure thing. Of course."

"It's just... it's the kind of thing you never would have done before the divorce."

"That's because I was an ass," said Reilly, chuckling wryly.

"Well, I don't know if I'd call you names." Janessa smiled too.

"In some ways, maybe the divorce has been a good thing," said Reilly.

"In some ways," she agreed. "See you around, Caius."

"See you around, Jannie."

* * *

"Hi," said Emmaline Campbell, holding out her hand to Wren. She was a pretty girl. Thin. Pale. But that was to be expected when she was battling cancer. She smiled at Wren, and her smile was almost too wide for her face, and it was infectious.

Wren couldn't help but smile too. She shook hands with Emmaline. "Hi."

"I wanted to meet you earlier," said Emmaline. "When I heard that you said yes, I said we should do something for you. Like have you over to dinner or something. But we haven't been in the mood for cooking lately, me and Mama, not after Oliver."

"It's absolutely fine," said Wren. "You don't have to do anything for me."

Alice Delacroix approached from the parking lot of the clinic where they had met up. She had been parking the car, but had dropped her daughter Emmaline off at the door. Wren had been waiting there for them.

She wasn't sure exactly why they were meeting up. It wasn't necessary for them to be there while she got blood drawn. Maybe they just wanted to make sure she'd actually do it. She thought that if it was someone she loved dying, and if some other person was her best hope for saving her loved one, she'd be pretty motivated to make sure too.

"Yes, we do," said Emmaline. "I do. If you can help me, I'll owe you."

"No," said Wren. "Absolutely not. It's the kind of thing that people do for each other. That, um, that..."

"Sisters?"

"Yeah, that sisters do." But Wren couldn't look the girl in the eye. *I am not doing this in penance. I didn't kill Oliver.*

Alice joined them. "Well, you made it, Wren. I'm glad."

"Of course," said Wren. "I said I'd be here. I am. You don't have to worry. I keep my promises."

"We're not worried," said Alice, forcing a laugh. She pointed to the door. "Shall we?"

They went into the clinic. Wren went to the front desk to sign in while Alice and Emmaline stood behind her, waiting. They gave her paperwork to fill out even though she wasn't really a patient. Wren went back to a chair and began to scribble and check boxes.

While she was doing that, Alice and Emmaline sat on either side and watched, both quiet.

Wren wanted to hide the paper from them for some reason. She felt nervous with their eyes on her. But she finished it quickly and returned it to the front desk.

When she came back to her seat, Alice said, "Do you know what to expect?"

"They're just going to draw some blood," said Wren. "Right?"

"Right," said Alice. "But if you're a match, you'll need to take some supplements and then they'll do a long harvesting session. It takes hours, and it can be uncomfortable—"

"It's fine," said Wren. "I said I would do it." She wasn't sure why she was so defensive.

"I'm sorry." Alice looked away.

"I'm sorry," said Wren.

And then a nurse called Wren's name.

She got up.

Alice got up too.

Emmaline shook her head at her mother. She smiled her big smile at Wren. "We'll be here when you get back."

Wren smiled back, but her smile felt forced. She crossed to the nurse and went back with her. The nurse weighed her and took her blood pressure and temperature and then sat down at a computer and began asking her all the questions that had been on the forms that Wren had filled out. Wren wasn't even sure why she'd bothered filling those out. She wasn't sure why this stuff was even important.

She answered as best she could, but some of the things she didn't know, like about her family history. She didn't know anything about Adrian Campbell's illnesses or propensity for various diseases.

"Date of last menstrual period?" chirped the nurse.

"Uh... I don't know," said Wren. She'd left it blank on the form.

"Give me an estimate then," said the nurse.

"Well..." Wren got out her phone and scrolled through the calendar. She furrowed her brow. "Uh, let's see, should have been about..." Wait, that couldn't be right. She glared at the nurse. "Why does this even matter? Why the twenty questions? Just take my damned blood."

"Well, if you were pregnant, you wouldn't be able to donate marrow. It wouldn't be safe for you or the baby."

"I'm not pregnant," said Wren. "I'm on the pill." Well, actually, she had that ring thing that you inserted once a month, because she was hell at remembering to take a pill every day. The ring was easier because she only had to remember to put it in. She had to admit that she usually only remembered to take the thing out whenever she started her period, and then she would put another one in after it was over.

"Okay," said the nurse. "So, give me a guess about your period, then?"

Wren looked down at her calendar and gave her a random date.

"The pill isn't a hundred percent, you know," said the nurse.

"I'm not pregnant," Wren growled.

* * *

Wren kept her birth control rings in the refrigerator, because that was where they were meant to be stored. When she got back home, she went to the fridge and counted them.

"Fuck," she said.
Then she went to the bathroom and checked. No ring.
"Fuck," she said again.
She began to pace in her bedroom. One stupid mistake in the middle of the night. Just one. She'd been half asleep. She hadn't been thinking clearly. And of *course*, she was going to pay for that stupid mistake. Of course.
Technically, she guessed it was three stupid mistakes.
Mistake number one: Forgetting to put in a new birth control ring.
Mistake number two: Forgetting to buy condoms at the grocery store.
Mistake number three: Unprotected sex with Hawk in the middle of the night when she was barely awake and still traumatized from being knocked out and put in a well.
She took out a ring and started to open the package.
But no.
She should probably not put that in now. Not if the damage was done.
She threw herself face down on her bed and pounded her fists into the mattress for several moments.
Then she got up, smoothed over the covers, and stalked out of her house. She sent Reilly a text saying that she wasn't going to make it in to work this afternoon after all. Then she got in her car and started it up. She pulled out on the road and headed for the interstate.
She drove.
She took one highway to another, ended up going south on I-95 for a long time. The traffic was bad and she was in a snarl of slow moving cars, all the lanes creeping along.
By the time she got to her destination, it was late.
She considered that the guy might not even be there. She didn't know if he'd moved or if he had a class or if there was some other reason why he might not be in his apartment. And it would just figure that after she'd been in a car for almost four hours, that he wouldn't be there, and she would

have wasted a trip.

But part of her almost hoped he wouldn't answer the door. She needed to know, but she didn't want to know.

She wanted to hide from this, the way she'd hidden from it already, even though she knew, she'd always known. In some ways, she'd been certain, deep down, certain since that night when she'd found Vada Walker's body.

She knocked at the door of Spencer Collins's apartment.

She waited.

Nothing.

She drew in a shaky breath, hoping for relief, but instead feeling a rising panic that threatened to strangle her. She needed him to be home. She needed to know. She wasn't certain after all. She only had suspicions.

She knocked again.

Immediately, the door opened.

Spencer Collins looked her over. "Oh, whoa," he said. "You're back."

"Hi," she said.

"Look, if you've been getting more calls—"

"I haven't," she said. Now, she was wondering why she hadn't simply called Spencer Collins instead of driving down here. She could have texted him a photo. She didn't need to be here in person. Maybe the long drive had been a delay tactic. Maybe—but he was looking expectantly at her. "That's not why I'm here. Well, it has something to do with why I'm here."

" You going to accuse me of murder again, because I thought you caught the guy."

She took out her phone. "I, um, I want to show you a picture."

"Okay," he said.

She had to hunt the picture down. She scrolled and clicked. "Um, when I was here before, you told us that there was a guy with you, someone who told you things about the Fellowship and the Crimson Ram. You said that he got you drunk and you didn't remember making the calls."

"Yeah," said Spencer.

"Was it this guy?"

Spencer looked. "No, not that guy. He's the one you arrested for the murders. Major Hill. I saw his picture on the TV. I know who he is. If it had been him, that would have been so freaky—"

"This guy?" She showed him another picture.

"That's David Song. You think I wouldn't recognize David Song?"

"Well, he'd be older now," she said. "And maybe he wouldn't have a beard. Maybe he'd..." She scrutinized the picture herself, wondering what David Song *would* look like older and without a beard.

"No, he wasn't old. I mean, he wasn't young or anything either. He was older, but not old, you know?"

She didn't. Not exactly. She showed him another picture. "What about this guy?"

Spencer swallowed. "Yeah. That's him."

Wren grimaced. Her voice squeaked a little. "You sure?"

"Positive," said Spencer. "That was him."

Wren put the phone in her pocket. "Thanks." She turned to go.

"Wait," called Spencer after her. "Who is that guy? Why did he come to me? What's this about?"

Wren kept walking.

CHAPTER ELEVEN

Reilly pulled on his jacket. He was standing at the door of Janessa's place, getting ready to leave. It was around 10:00 that night.

She was taking off her jacket. "He go to sleep okay?"

"Yeah, went great," said Reilly. "We had a lot of fun."

"Thanks for doing this, Caius," she said. "When my sitter backed out at the last minute, I didn't know who else to call."

"Like I said, happy to do it," said Reilly. "I didn't have anything going on, and I'm always up for seeing the little guy." He had to admit that now that the first rush of joy over connection with Timmy had waned, what he felt now primarily was guilt. All along, his little boy had been in there, reachable, and he hadn't tried to reach him.

How many years had he missed due to his ignorance and idiocy? How much further along could Timmy be? He worried too that they'd missed the prime years for Timmy's language acquisition. He was too old now, his brain didn't have the same elasticity as a two-year-old.

Of course, it may not have made much difference. Maybe Timmy wouldn't have been ready as a toddler. But they didn't know. They couldn't know. And they couldn't go back.

Anyway, any time he could spend with his son now, he wanted it. Not only because he loved his kid, but because he had so much to try to make up for. So, when Janessa had called last minute and asked if he wanted to come over to feed Timmy dinner and put him to bed, he'd jumped on it right away.

"I know you are," said Janessa. "And I'm glad."

"Me too," he said.

There was an awkward moment, and then he headed for the door. "Well, give me a call if you need me to do it again."

"Okay, I'll do that."

He opened the door, and then he paused and turned back to her. "Hey, Jannie?"

"Yeah?"

"What's the next step?" he said.

"What do you mean?"

"I mean, I read that book, and I get how kids are supposed to start breaking down the gestalts, how if he gets to the next stage, he'll start mixing up the quotes from *Thomas*, putting them together with other quotes. But what I don't get from the book is how to get him there."

"Yeah," said Janessa, making a face. "That part isn't very clear to me either."

He shut the door. "The first part has seemed so easy, and he's a different kid already. It's like, he didn't realize anyone cared about anything he said and now that he knows, he's communicating so much more. Or maybe he was communicating all along, and we just didn't understand. So, just for that, I think the book is brilliant. But it's not much of a step-by-step thing."

"I think it's more descriptive," she said. "I think the kid has to sort of naturally acquire the language. That's why it's called obtaining language naturally."

"Yeah, but if he could have naturally obtained language, he already would have," said Reilly. "Should we model it for him? Should we break up gestalts ourselves?"

Janessa spread her hands. "*I* have been."

"Oh, good, because I did too," he said. "I don't know if that's just going to make him copy what we're saying as new gestalts, though? I mean, is that bad?"

"I don't know." She shrugged. "I guess we just wait. And talk to him as much as we can and engage with him. I think the more he realizes that language is a way to engage with other people, the more he'll be motivated to use it with us. I mean, I hope so."

"I hope so, too."

"When you think about what language is, it kind of has to come from Timmy. Anything else would only be him saying things he'd memorized, which is what he's good at. He needs space and freedom to form words on his own, and we have to be there to foster his growth, not force it."

"I'm not trying to force anything."

"I know. I don't have the answers either," she said.

"I guess... it's easy to want it all, you know?" he said. "I had just gotten to this place where I had mostly accepted Timmy for what he was, and it wasn't much. And then I realized that I was selling him short. So, now, I'm getting more than I'd thought I could have, but... how much can we hope for?"

"We hope for the moon, Caius," she said.

"Yeah?"

"Yeah," she said. "And when it hurts too much to hope, we take a break for a little bit until we have it in us to hope again."

* * *

Reilly was scribbling his signature on one of a stack of documents in the prison where Vivian Delacroix was being kept.

It wasn't too far away from Cardinal Falls. They'd had about a forty minute drive, during which Wren had kept starting to say something and then stopping, telling him it was nothing. It was driving him crazy. He wished she'd just spit it out. But he figured she was nervous about seeing her mother, so he was giving her a pass.

He flipped the page to the next one, scanned to the

bottom and signed again. Paperwork.

"Initial here," said the guard who was working there. She pointed at a spot on the piece of paper.

Reilly initialed. He flipped the page. He signed the bottom. That was the last page. He looked at the guard. "Good?"

The guard took the documents and flipped through them. "Good." She set the papers aside. "You need to leave all your weapons behind here."

Reilly took his gun out, unloaded it, and handed it over.

The guard looked at Wren, who was chewing on her bottom lip.

"She doesn't have anything," said Reilly.

"Okay," said the guard. "Well, it's through there." She pointed to a thick, metal door.

Reilly headed over.

Wren hesitated and then joined him.

The guard buzzed them through the door.

They went through and emerged in a small room where another guard was sitting. He waved them through, and then they had to wait to be buzzed through another set of doors.

"Down the hall, second door on the right," the guard called after them.

They proceeded down a narrow hall with no windows, the light overhead bright and fluorescent.

Reilly opened the second door and they entered a small room with a table in the center. No one was in there. There were two chairs on the side next to the door, and one chair on the other side. There was a bolt on the table to attach chains to.

Reilly shut the door and pulled out one of the chairs. It screeched against the floor. He sat down and scooted it noisily in.

Wren stayed standing, chewing on her lip.

He looked up at her. "You all right?"

"I went to see Spencer Collins yesterday."

"Who?"

"You remember," she said. "When I was still at the FBI Academy, I got phone calls from a guy claiming to be David Song?"

"Oh, right," said Reilly. "That guy in Richmond? Why'd you go to see him?"

"Well, we never... he said that there was another man who came and who got him drunk and that while he was drunk, the calls were made from his phone. We speculated that maybe the man who made them was the killer. That maybe it was connected to me somehow. The killer wanted me back in Cardinal Falls. And then we caught Major, and he supposedly had a thing for me, and that was why the girls were the age that I was when I was an initiate."

"Yeah, I remember this," said Reilly.

"But we never went and asked him if it was Major who came to see him."

"No," said Reilly. "We didn't. I guess it didn't seem important. We didn't need that information in order to prove that it was Major. But I can see why it might put your mind at ease to go there. So, did you to talk to Spencer?"

"I did. I showed him Major's picture."

"And?"

"And he said it wasn't him," said Wren.

"Huh," said Reilly. "Well—"

"It was Hawk," said Wren.

He turned to her sharply, his mind reeling.

But then the door opened and two guards brought Vivian Delacroix into the room.

CHAPTER TWELVE

Wren's heart stopped at the sight of her. She hadn't seen her mother in fifteen years, and then, only at the sentencing, from across the room. Her father Hayes had tried to encourage her to go over to see Vivian, to say goodbye, but Wren didn't want to. She remembered that Vivian hadn't even looked at her during the sentencing anyway. Vivian had been too interested in looking at the cameras.

Vivian looked older. Her hair was streaked with gray, and her face was weathered. But her face was familiar, and Wren knew her. Seeing her, it made her chest tight.

She sat down in one of the chairs as the guards hooked Vivian's cuffed hands to the hook in the table, her cuffed ankles to the floor.

All the while, Vivian looked straight at her. Her eyes were shining.

Wren wanted to look away, but she couldn't. She was fixed by the gaze, and everything else in the room seemed to fall away. She only realized that the guards had left the room when she heard the door close. The sound of its clicking shut made her jump.

"Wren," said Vivian. "Wren, my little girl. You're so grown up."

Wren licked her lips.

"When I heard you were coming to see me, I couldn't believe it," said Vivian. Tears were starting to spill out of her eyes. "After all this time. I had given up hope of ever getting to see you again. Thank you for coming."

Wren looked down at the table. Her voice was dull and flat. "You said you have information for us. Start talking."

"This must be Detective Renley?" said Vivian.

"Reilly," said Reilly in a low voice.

"I never thought you'd work with law enforcement, Wren, sweetie." Vivian laughed a little. "If I'd been there while you were growing up—"

"Well, you weren't," said Wren. "And let's not do this, okay? You don't need to pretend with me. I know you."

"What are you talking about?" Vivian's voice was gentle, melodious. It was the voice Wren had always imagined to hear from a mother after a scraped knee or a broken heart. It was funny that Vivian was so good at faking that voice. "I'm not pretending, sweetie. I missed you so much. You are the most important person in the world to me—"

"You had my father killed," said Wren. "Why'd you do that before I ever got the chance to meet him?"

"Hayes? Hayes is dead?"

"You know that Hayes isn't my father," said Wren. "Adrian Campbell is. Was. But then you sent people out to kill him—"

"Listen, baby girl, I don't even know where to start, but the things they say about me, they aren't true. Wren, sweetie, you were *there*. You know that I never told anyone to kill anyone."

Wren sat back in her chair and gaped at Vivian. "Seriously? You're going to deny everything?" Then she laughed a dry laugh. "Oh, of course, you never really did admit it. But what's the point now, Vivian? Your appeals, they've all been shot down. Why lie?"

"I'm not lying." Vivian's voice broke. "I said things, and my words got twisted, and then—"

"We're not here for this either," said Wren, nostrils flaring. She stood up from the table. "Do you have information for us or not?"

"Maybe I just wanted to see you. Maybe I knew that

there was no other way to get you to see me. Maybe—"

"So, you lied. Well, big surprise." Wren was sarcastic.

"I didn't lie," said her mother. "I think you arrested the wrong man for the murders of those little girls. Major Hill would never have it in him to do that."

"Right, so who did?" said Wren.

"Hawk Marner, of course," said Vivian, the corners of her lips turning up slightly, as if saying this out loud satisfied her.

Wren's jaw twitched.

Reilly cleared his throat. "Why would you accuse Mr. Marner, Ms. Delacroix?"

"Just... call it intuition," said Vivian, turning to Reilly. "Hawk's mother abandoned him. I practically raised him."

Wren snorted.

"Mother's intuition," said Vivian in a silken voice, ignoring Wren.

Wren got up from the table. "We're done here."

"Oh, wait, please don't go, Wren." Vivian reached out a shackled hand toward her daughter.

"Wren," said Reilly. "Let's find out what she knows."

"You heard her," said Wren. "Intuition. She's got nothing. And anyway, I don't need to hear this. I already knew this. Before we came in here, I *told* you—"

"Just wait," said Reilly.

"Wren," said Vivian. "Don't leave. You have the wrong idea about me. I could never have orchestrated all this death and pain. I don't know why you would think that about me, when all I ever showed you was unconditional love. Honestly, I miss you so much. If you would consider just visiting me once in a while, so that I can see you—"

"Stop," said Wren.

"I think about you all the time," whispered Vivian.

It was quiet in the room.

"You were always so close to Hawk," said Vivian. "You never saw him clearly."

"Stop," Wren said again.
"You don't see me clearly either," said Vivian.
Wren shot across the room to the door. She yanked it open.
"Hey," said Reilly. "Wait."
Wren didn't.

* * *

By the time Reilly made it out of the prison, Wren was out in the parking lot. She was talking to someone who was standing next to his car, and then Reilly saw the man give Wren a cigarette. Wren lit the thing with shaking hands and then handed him back his lighter.

Reilly took a deep breath and then started across the parking lot to her.

When he got to her, she was coughing out smoke.

"Nasty habit," he said softly.

She coughed and then took a drag. "I'm out of practice," she managed before another coughing fit overtook her.

Reilly snatched the cigarette out of her hand and tossed it to the ground. He started to step on it, but she pushed him out of the way.

She bent over to pick up the cigarette, and her purse slipped off her shoulder. It overturned and things spilled all over the pavement. "Fuck," said Wren in a defeated voice. Cigarette abandoned, she gazed down at all her belongings on the ground.

Reilly got to his knees and started picking things up.

In a moment, she joined him.

She shoved her keys back into her purse. A tube of lipstick. Her wallet.

Reilly picked up a tin of mints. A pen. Some kind of small box, which he didn't look at until he was handing it over to her, and then he realized what it was.

They locked gazes over it, her hands closing on the box of pregnancy tests just as the realization of it all washed over him. They both held onto it and stared at each other.

A moment passed.

Two.

He let go of the box.

She put it back in her purse.

He looked around for anything else that had fallen out. He retrieved two more pens and a hair tie and gave them to her. Then, without meeting her gaze, he went over to the driver's side of the car and got in.

Seconds later, she got in the passenger's side and slammed the door shut.

He pulled out of the parking lot.

CHAPTER THIRTEEN

"Uh..." Reilly stared over Angela's shoulder at the chalkboard proclaiming the specials in the Daily Bean. "Do you have anything without, um, caffeine?"

"I want caffeine, you asshole," snarled Wren from behind him. She shoved him out of the way. "I can order my own drink." She looked at Angela. "I want, um, I want—"

"Should you have caffeine, though?" said Reilly. "I mean, it's been awhile since I went through this with Janessa, but I remember that she didn't do coffee—"

"Shut. Up." Wren glared at him.

Reilly shoved his hands in his pockets and looked at his shoes.

Wren turned back to Angela. "You made me this salt thing once?"

"A sea salt coffee?"

"Yeah," said Wren. "I remember saying I could stand to do one of those again."

"Coming right up," said Angela. "You okay?"

"I'm fine," said Wren. "I'm absolutely fucking fine."

Angela winced a little at the expletive.

"Sorry," Wren muttered.

"I'll get you your coffee," said Angela. She smiled at Reilly. "Ginger latte? Triple shot?"

"Yeah," he said. "Same as always." He glanced at Wren. "Listen, Wren, I think we need—"

"Not in here," she whispered.

He nodded. "Okay."

And then they were quiet again, as quiet as they'd been on the drive over, during which he hadn't asked if she wanted to get coffee. He'd just driven here. It wasn't until he'd pulled in that he'd thought of the caffeine problem.

Moments passed.

Finally, the coffee was ready, and they went back to Reilly's car.

They got inside, and he didn't start the car. He drank his coffee. "Wren, just because Hawk went to that Spencer guy, it doesn't mean that he's a killer."

"It does," said Wren.

"It only means that he..." Reilly drank more coffee. "Okay, so he drove all the way to Richmond and targeted some random guy to get his phone, and then what, made him call—"

"Hawk used Spencer's phone. He called me himself," she said. "When I think about it now, I recognize his voice. I recognized it all along, I think, in the back of my head. But I didn't—I couldn't let myself—make the connection."

"Okay, but still, that doesn't mean that he killed anyone."

"He wanted me back in Cardinal Falls," she said. "I think he thought that if I came back, he could stop."

"But there's no evidence—"

"He always says these weird things to be about how I make him better, but then yesterday, he said that he was wrong. It wasn't true. Because when he killed Oliver, he killed him *for* me. He can't stop, not even with me around."

"There were two more bodies after you returned to town. What does it have to do with your being around?"

"Vada was killed before I had seen Hawk," she said. "And Jenny Smith was different, remember? The body with the face covered? I said that it was regret, that the killer was ashamed of what he did. And that night, it was the first night that Hawk and I were... together."

Reilly looked away. "That's circumstantial."

"Why are you suddenly his fan club? I didn't think you liked him. You said he was creepy."

"I'm not his fan club," said Reilly. "I just don't want this to be true… for you. Especially with…" He gestured at her coffee cup, as if that was somehow related.

"I don't want it to be true either," she said.

"So, maybe it isn't," he said.

"He gave wine to a little girl at my father's wedding."

"You think that means…?"

"The murders are about being sexually attracted to girls that age. He's admitted to me that he was attracted to me when I was too young for him to be attracted to me. He…" She swallowed. "It's always been him, and I've known it since I ran into him after I found Vada's body. He was out in the woods, watching the police bag it up, because killers do that. They like to see the effects of their handiwork."

Reilly didn't say anything.

She sipped at her coffee.

"That, um, that good? The sea salt thing?"

"You run out of things to say to try to convince me that I'm wrong?"

"I just… I had a thought," said Reilly.

"What?" she said.

"Did you, uh, did you talk to Hawk about the case with Noah Adams?"

"A little bit, at the end. I told him that we needed evidence to prove that he did it. I might have even said that finding the gun he used would have helped. I know that probably wasn't the responsible thing to do, but sometimes it's hard to shut it all off."

"No, I get it. I'm not chastising you."

"So, why bring it up?"

"You, uh, you said that he killed Oliver *for* you."

"Yeah, so?"

"Well, I'm just thinking about Noah Adams."

"Noah killed himself."

"Yeah, he did," said Reilly. "But I watched Hawk talk Colt Baldwin into turning the shotgun on himself."

"Wait, what?" She slammed her coffee cup into the cup holder. "What the hell? How do you talk someone into killing themselves?"

"He just... did it," said Reilly. "I told you, he's creepy."

"And you think he did the same thing to Noah Adams?"

Reilly spread his hands. "I don't know. It probably doesn't matter. I doubt you could prosecute him for it. It's pretty obvious that Noah pulled the trigger himself. Hawk told me that you couldn't talk someone into it unless they already wanted to."

"Oh, so you guys talked technique? What the hell, Reilly, why didn't you tell me this before?"

"I..." He started the car. "I don't know. Maybe I didn't want to face how I felt about him."

"Why not?"

"I don't know." He was defensive about it, and he didn't know why that was either.

"Because with me, it makes sense, but I don't see why you'd have some vested interest in keeping him pure as the driven snow."

"I don't. Actually, he's rubbed me the wrong way since the very beginning. I've never liked him."

"So, then, why?"

"Well, it doesn't make sense, me not liking him." Reilly tore out of the parking lot, throwing Wren back against her seat.

"Geez, watch the coffee," she said, reaching out to protect it.

"I thought maybe I didn't like him just because you had some thing with him."

"Why should that matter?"

"It shouldn't," he snapped.

She glanced at him and then quickly away.

"It doesn't." His voice was quieter. "It doesn't at all."

CHAPTER FOURTEEN

"Look, let me do it," Reilly said. He was standing inside Wren's office.

"No," she said, toying with her phone. "It has to be me."

"It doesn't have to be you. It shouldn't be you. You're too connected to him. We have to turn the entire case over to other people. We're both compromised at this point. You're involved with him. I know him socially. We should get someone else in here right away, have them do it."

"No one else knows the case like we do," she said.

"What you're saying is that Hawk completely changed his victim type—"

"For me," she said. "The other victims, I think they were substitutes for me in some way. But now, he has me. The real me. He thought that would be enough to stem his urge to kill, but when it wasn't, he just twisted his killing so that it would be about me in some way. It's always been about me. It still is."

"This the kind of thing that you study in the FBI? There a profile for this?"

"No," she said. "No, he doesn't fit at all."

"But you're convinced."

"I don't want to be convinced. I want something to prove to me that it isn't him at all, and that he's innocent. That's what I want."

"Yeah, and then you and Hawk can start decorating a nursery together."

"Don't," she said, shaking her head at him.

"Sorry," he said. He dragged a hand over the top of his head. "This is all extremely fucked up, you recognize that, right?"

"I need it to be me, because he'll suspect anyone else." She pointed. "Go out into the hall. I can't look at you while I'm doing it. It'll mess me up."

"Wren…" He sighed.

"Maybe he'll have an alibi."

"You know he doesn't."

"Maybe he'll say something that will prove it's not him."

He sucked in a breath and then he did as she said. He went out into the hallway.

Wren dialed him on her phone.

Hawk picked up on the second ring. "Little bird? Haven't heard from you in a few days."

"I know," she said. "I've been busy with work." Did she sound normal? Would he hear anything suspicious in her voice? "Actually, that's why I'm calling. I need you to do me a big favor and come down to headquarters so that we can talk to you again about some of Major's murders and also about Oliver. Major's recanting his confession, and he's pointing the finger at you. I just need to make sure we go over it again so that there's no question of your guilt if anyone else would look into it. Do you think you could do that for me?"

"Sure, no problem," said Hawk. "You think we could do something tonight? Maybe dinner? Maybe not burgers at the bait and tackle shop?"

She forced a laugh out of her lips. "You mean, an actual date, Hawk? I don't know."

"Come on, say yes. One date won't kill you."

"Okay," she said. "Sure. We can do dinner."

"Excellent," he said. "I'll be down to headquarters in the next ten minutes."

* * *

But he never showed up.

They waited twenty minutes, Wren pacing almost the entire time, her heart in her throat.

Then they waited ten more minutes. This time, Wren sat in a chair in her office, feeling a sense of dread surround her.

She called Hawk again, then, because he was late.

He didn't answer.

"I fucked up," she muttered. "I tipped him off somehow. He knew, and he ran."

"That's crazy, Wren," said Reilly. "I heard you. You sounded completely normal."

"It's because I agreed to the date," said Wren. "I would never do that. I don't go out on dates with him. I'm always pushing him away. And the other night, when he came by, I made him leave, because the suspicions were boiling over inside me, and he must have sensed that something was wrong. He asked me out as a test. If everything had been okay, I would have turned him down flat. Damn it, I fucked up."

Reilly shook his head at her. "You have a really weird relationship with this guy."

"It's not a relationship," she said.

"Sorry," he said. "I don't know why I said that."

"And you know what else?" she said. "He's been trying to pin Oliver's death on me. He kept making these hints, little jibes here and there, and damned if it wasn't working. I was starting to believe it."

"Yeah," said Reilly. "He did that to me too."

"He was playing us," said Wren. She shook her head, laughing helplessly. "He's exactly like my mother."

"You know, we still haven't talked about that," said Reilly. "This has been a really traumatic day for you, and—"

"Stop," said Wren.

"I'm only saying that maybe we don't need to go full speed ahead. Or maybe you should go home and relax a little bit and leave things to me and the team."

"The uniforms? Are you kidding? You need me." She got

up from her chair, picking up her purse. " No, I was only saying stop, because I'm going to go to the bathroom."

"Oh," said Reilly. "Okay. Hurry back."

She swept out of the office.

CHAPTER FIFTEEN

Wren splashed water on her face and stared at her reflection in the mirror.

She got the pregnancy test out of her purse and opened the box. She pulled out one of the individually-wrapped tests. There were more than one in there. They seemed to only come in packs of two or three. She pulled out the directions and read them.

She started to open one of the tests.

Then she shoved it back in the box and stuck the box back in her purse.

She left the bathroom.

Reilly was still in her office.

She stopped in the doorway.

"You all right?" he said.

"Let's go," she said.

"Go?'

"We need to find Hawk," she said. "I'm telling you, he ran."

"Try calling him again," said Reilly, but he came out of her office into the hallway.

She tried to find her phone in her purse, but she couldn't. There were too many stupid things in there, and she started yanking things out, including the stupid pregnancy test. What did she care? It wasn't like Reilly hadn't seen it already.

Now, everything was weird with them, and she didn't like it.

But then again, there was basically nothing about this situation she liked.

No phone.

She shoved everything back into her phone. "I can't find my phone."

"I'll call it," said Reilly, getting his own phone out of his pocket.

Her phone rang. It was on her desk. She scooped it up, silencing the ringing. She called Hawk again. No answer. She shook her head at Reilly.

"All right," he said. "Let's go. Maybe he didn't run. Maybe he had car trouble."

"And didn't call?"

"Maybe his phone ran out of battery or he's in a spot where there's no service."

"Maybe," she conceded.

"But we should still look for him. Try to clear this up," said Reilly. "You know, if we do find him, and he is trying to run, we can't arrest him or anything."

"I bet if we get him talking, he'll confess," said Wren. "He feels guilty about what he's done."

"Or he did," said Reilly. "Maybe there was some kind of turning point before Oliver and Noah. He changed his MO radically, and now he's doing it altruistically, for you. That's not the kind of thing that people feel guilty about. If your theory is right, and I'm not saying I entirely understand it, then he might be proud of himself now."

"Either way, he'll talk," said Wren. "At the very least, if anyone's got a chance of getting him to talk, it's going to be me."

"Well, you're probably right about that," said Reilly.

They got back in Reilly's car and they drove to the compound. The first place they went was Hawk's cabin. He wasn't there. Neither was his car. The door was unlocked, and they went inside. The place was messy, and that bothered her. She'd always thought that Major's neatness matched the psychology of the killer better. Maybe she was wrong about everything.

"Why were the trophies at Major's place if Hawk did all of it?" said Reilly.

"Well, I found the first trophy at Hawk's," she said. "And then he left, ostensibly to go warn Major."

"And it took us a while to get there to Major's place," said Reilly. "They were both gone."

"Giving Hawk ample time to plant them."

"You think he took trophies from Oliver and Noah?" said Reilly.

She strode over to Hawk's couch, where she'd found the ID card for Jenny Smith. She upturned the cushions, and there, tucked in a crevice in the couch, was a small wooden box. Much smaller than the one at Major's, but similar in design.

"Damn," said Reilly. "It really is him."

"Gloves," said Wren. "We shouldn't touch it."

"In the car," said Reilly. "I'll get them."

"No, let me," said Wren, and she fled out of the house. She had jumped Hawk on that couch. They'd kissed there. They'd had sex. She gulped at the fresh air out here, feeling sick to her stomach.

But feeling queasy? The implications of that? That was another twist of the knife.

She flung open the door to Reilly's car and got out his evidence kit. Gloves and baggies. She brought it inside.

"Why'd he put it in the same place that you found it before?" said Reilly.

"I don't know," she said. "I guess force of habit. Serial killers ritualize things. If they don't do it the same way, it doesn't feel the same." She pulled on a pair of gloves. She picked up the box. She opened it.

It was empty.

She let out a little cry and let it fall.

Reilly had gloves on now. He picked it up. "Huh. Maybe

it's just a box."

"Maybe he took the trophies when he ran," said Wren.

They looked through the rest of the house. They didn't find anything incriminating, but then that might have been a good thing, since they hadn't gotten a warrant for Hawk's house. They'd only come in to look for him, or to look for signs that he'd left.

After they'd looked through everything, they went back out to Reilly's car and drove around the compound, asking if anyone had seen him.

No one had.

Then, out on the northern edge of the compound, near the meeting house, they found Hawk's car, but Hawk wasn't in it.

Isaac Scott was trimming some hedges outside the meeting house. He waved at them. "Hi there!"

Wren and Reilly trudged over to him.

"Isaac, did you see Hawk park this car?" called Wren.

"Wren, did you ever talk to the Daramonds?" said Isaac.

"Did he get out? Is he in the meeting house?" said Wren. "Did you talk to him?"

"Did the Daramonds confirm my alibi?" said Isaac.

Wren sighed. "Yes, okay, the Daramonds said you were there. You're not a suspect. You happy?"

"I'm relieved," said Isaac.

"Hawk?" said Wren.

"Don't know anything about that car," said Isaac. "I went inside the meeting house earlier, and it wasn't there. When I came back out, it was. Didn't see Hawk anywhere."

"Huh," said Wren, mostly to herself.

"Where could he have gone?" said Reilly.

"Maybe out in the woods?" spoke up Isaac.

The woods?

Great. There were acres and acres of woods out there. And Hawk had shown himself adept at doing things amongst the trees, since that had been his kill site for the girls.

"Who would know where Hawk goes in the woods?" said Reilly.

"Major," said Wren. "Major went with him everywhere."

* * *

"So, if this is true, then Major is innocent," said Reilly.

They were back at jail for the second time that day, only a different jail. Major was being held in Martinsburg, because he was awaiting his trial. Vivian Delacroix, on the other hand, had been sentenced and was held in a maximum security prison elsewhere. Seeing Major was less of a hassle than seeing Vivian, but they were here without any advanced notice, so they had to wait until the prison could arrange for them to talk to Major.

"Yeah," said Wren. "I guess they'd let him go, then?"

"Right," said Reilly. "But I got to tell you, Wren, we don't have the evidence we need for Hawk."

"I know," she said. "But it's him. Major's telling the truth, and Hawk did all of this. We'll find the evidence."

"You're sure of that now? We were going to talk to him to try to find some reason to prove that he didn't do it."

"That was before he ran."

"Right," said Reilly. He sighed.

She sighed.

He tapped his fingers against the chair where he was sitting.

She sat up straight. "Is there a bathroom in here?"

Reilly pointed. "I remember this from Janessa. She was peeing constantly. It's got something to do with blood flow—"

"What are you talking about?" said Wren.

Reilly hesitated. "Nothing."

"I don't even need to go," Wren muttered. "I was just… I was going to go and … I've been carrying that stupid pregnancy test around with me all day, and…"

"Oh," said Reilly. "Well, you should probably do that. It'

s actually a good idea. Knowing for certain would be good for you."

"Yeah, I don't know about that," she said.

Reilly nodded. "Okay, then."

Wren leaned back against the wall and shut her eyes. "I'd be a really terrible mother, Reilly."

"What?" He turned to her. "That's crazy. You'd be great."

She opened one eye.

"I mean..." He shrugged. "There's not a lot to it."

She shut her eyes again and snorted. "You met my mother today."

"Right," said Reilly.

"That's not what she's like."

"What do you mean?"

"It was all an act," said Wren. "I used to watch her do that. She'd turn it on for people, for whoever she needed to manipulate. But she never bothered using it on me. I wasn't important. It wasn't until today that she tried it on me."

Reilly wasn't sure how to respond to that, so he didn't.

"It kind of made me feel a little special. It means she cares, in some way. It means she deemed me important enough of a person to try to get something from me."

"What do you think she wanted?"

"Whatever she could get. Money maybe. The way I understand it, it's very expensive to be in jail. There's a whole crazy economy going on in there. Maybe she wanted access to things on the outside. I don't think anyone visits her." She opened her eyes. "Maybe she was just lonely. Even psychopaths get lonely."

"That what you think Vivian is?"

"I know it," said Wren. "It was so easy to recognize the type when I was in the Academy because I saw my mother do that sort of thing my whole life. I know she's nothing but cold."

"Yeah, but that doesn't mean you'd be that sort of a

mother."

"I don't know," said Wren. "Sometimes, I wonder if I'm just like her."

"You're not," said Reilly. "Don't say things like that."

"What about me distinguishes me so much from Vivian Delacroix?"

"You have nothing in common with her. You're not a cult leader."

"No," she said. "But I do seem to spend all of my free time thinking about murder."

"Not the same, Wren, come on."

She studied her fingernails. "Maybe not the same. Maybe slightly better, but—"

"Look at me," he said.

She raised her gaze slowly.

"We are the good guys, okay? We stop the bad guys. There's nothing about what we do that's remotely similar to what murderers do."

"But we have to understand them," said Wren. "I *like* to understand them. I'm fascinated by all of it. Besides, have you seen me? I can't even take care of myself. I wear the same jeans every day. I don't know how to cook. I'm not… I can't do it, okay? There's no freaking way."

"If you have to, you'll step up. You're extremely capable," he said. "It'll be okay."

"I don't think anything is going to be okay, ever again."

CHAPTER SIXTEEN

"There's a place out in the woods that we built together," Major said. He was happy to see them both, eager for them to believe what he'd said before, that Hawk was guilty, not him. He took the fact that they were asking questions about Hawk as a good sign.

It was, but Wren didn't want him to get his hopes up. She wasn't sure how to feel about Major. It was pretty likely that he was collateral damage, manipulated and twisted by Hawk for his own ends. But it was also possible that he'd been very involved. Maybe the two of them had done the girls together. Or maybe she was wrong about Hawk.

She still wanted to be wrong about Hawk, but she couldn't make herself believe it was true.

"A place," she repeated. "Like a house?"

"Not a nice house," said Major. "No glass in the windows. No electricity or anything like that. We built it ourselves. We dragged things out from the compound. We took wood and nails and tools. We had to make a path between the trees. We did that first. We went through and hacked out a path, and then we had to keep it clear so that we could go back and forth."

"Is this near where the bones were?" Wren said. "Where the girls were killed?"

Major shook his head. "No. I didn't like that place. That was Hawk's place."

"But you knew all about it," said Wren.

"I knew it because Hawk wanted me to know it. Because

he was trying to set me up," said Major. "He had planned for me to be his scapegoat all along, you know? It makes me so mad when I think about it. I thought we were friends. But he just used me. He saw me as weak and impressionable. He didn't care about me at all."

"But you confessed," Wren said. "How does someone get another person to confess to murder of all things? How could Hawk ever have been able to convince you of that?"

"You've met him," said Major. "He can do that. I think it's because he's still in touch with the Crimson Ram. He says that the Crimson Ram gets in through the cracks—the ones between sleep and awake? The Horned Lord crawls through those cracks and he takes over. He's powerful too. He's a god."

"There's no such thing as the Crimson Ram," said Wren. "He's made up. What Hawk does, it isn't magic."

Major leaned forward. "But you agree that Hawk can do something, don't you?"

Reilly cleared his throat. "I think we're getting off track here. This house in the woods you built?"

"Right," said Major. "We worked on it for a long time. It took us months and months to make it. First we made the foundation. We dragged in concrete blocks on that litter we made. We dragged them over the path in the woods. It took a lot of trips. Then we set them up and then we built around it with wood. We framed it out and then we made the floor—"

"Where is it?" said Reilly. "Where's this house?"

"Is this where the two of you went before?" said Wren. "Right before you were arrested?"

"Yes, yes," Major said, nodding. "Hawk said no one would look for us there and that we could sneak out in the night and run away and I could start another life. But I didn't want that. He was making up lies about me."

"Except you didn't know that at the time, you believed the lies," said Wren.

"Some part of me always knew the truth," said Major. "I always knew that I could never have killed little girls like that. I'm not a monster like he is. I'm not crazy and evil. I don't talk to the Horned Lord. No, no, no. That's Hawk. That was always Hawk. He made me think that I was him, but I was *never* him."

"Major, where's the house in the woods?" said Reilly.

"You follow the path," said Major.

"The path that we followed to get to where the stone circle was?" said Wren. "That path?"

"No, a different path."

"How do we get to that path?"

"You go out towards where the crazies live," said Major. "But you don't go too close, because they'll get you if you get too close. You go past them, and then, the path is there."

"I don't know where that is," said Wren.

"Who are the crazies?" said Reilly.

"You don't know about the crazies?" said Major. "Really? Well, you don't want to know. They're worse than Hawk. They're real bad. They'll kill you and cut you up."

"And they live in the woods?" said Wren.

Major nodded urgently. "If you don't know where they live, you better not go out there, not by yourselves. You'll need me to come with you. I can show you where the crazies live, and help you stay away from them. And then I can show you the path to the house that Hawk and I made. But you'll have to get me out of here."

Wren sighed. "Major, we really can't do that."

"Why not? You know that it was Hawk, not me."

"We don't know that," said Wren. "All the evidence points to you, and you confessed. The fact that you're changing your story now—"

"You *do* know it was him," said Major. "I can tell. I can see it all over you. You know what it was that you were kissing, Wren. You were kissing the monster in the burning forest, and he's going to chew you up and spit you out now."

"Just tell us," said Wren. "Tell us how to get to the path and the house."

"No," said Major, putting his arms over his chest. "No, you get me out of here. Get me out and I'll show you. You know I'm innocent. Get me out of here *now*."

* * *

"I feel even more confused now than I did before I went in there," Wren muttered, scrunched down in the passenger's seat of Reilly's car. She was staring out the window.

"That's because you let yourself get out in the weeds with him. We were trying to get one little piece of information, and he wanted to talk. If you would have gone for it, instead of leading him down those little side paths that he wanted to go down, maybe we'd be further along than we are."

"What? Seriously? I was trying to make this all make sense. One of them did it, you know. And if it really was Hawk, I need to know how."

"No, you can't trust Major. He's not all there," said Reilly.

"No, I know," she said. "He's… off. And I don't know if that's because he's a murderer or because he was systematically broken down by Hawk so that he would be impressionable enough to use."

"You think Hawk could do that?"

"I think he was trying to do it to me," she said. "The thing with Oliver, getting into my head and making me think I could be capable…" She grimaced. "Maybe he's already been working on breaking me down, too. Maybe I don't even know all the things that—"

"You're giving him too much power. Stop thinking of him like that, like some kind of all-seeing, all-knowing entity. He's just a guy, and he's nothing special."

"Oh, whatever," she muttered.

"Wren, I'm serious. You—"

"*Could* we get Major out of jail?"

"What? Of course not. How could you possibly ask that?"

"Well, if we had evidence that Hawk did it, like irrefutable evidence?"

"Maybe," said Reilly. "Maybe then. But what we'd need would be DNA and a confession at this point. The case against Major is strong."

"But none of the evidence really ties to Major. They found the clothes and the bags and everything out in the woods, but they never found Major's DNA. They found the victims' DNA, but not his."

"Look, I'm not the person to argue this with."

"We need to find Hawk."

"Yes," said Reilly. "We do. And he's probably out there in that house, but we'll have to find it ourselves."

"There's no way we'll find it. Covering every inch of those woods would take too long. We need Major to guide us. What if we could get him out of jail to help out? Like a day outing."

"A day outing?"

"People get released from jail for special events sometimes. For a wedding or for a funeral or that sort of thing. Major isn't convicted of anything. He's being held without bail because of the seriousness of the charge. He's still awaiting trial. If we tell them it's possible he's even innocent, wouldn't someone loan him to us for a day?"

"I don't think so, Delacroix."

"Well, can't you ask?" Her voice was steadily rising.

"Ask who?"

"I don't know. Whoever it is you would ask in this situation. Lopez, maybe. He's your direct superior, right? Ask him." She gesticulated as her voice got even louder.

"It's a crazy request, and there's no way it's going to happen." As if in response, he got quieter, more still. His voice was a soft rumble in the car.

"Well, okay," she said. "But if you don't ask, you don't know!"

"Wren—"

"We *have* to find Hawk." And her voice was shrill now.

"Listen, why don't you calm down, okay?" His voice was softer still.

"Stop the car," she said.

"What?"

"Stop the car!" She pounded both fists on the dashboard.

Reilly, confused, pulled the car over to the side of the road.

Wren threw open the door and leaped out.

"Hey, Wren, what the fuck are you doing?" he called after her.

She took off running. They were on a country road, but there were houses on either side of the road. She ran through the yard of one house and then into a nearby field.

"Wren!" he called.

She didn't even look back.

Reilly muttered swear words under his breath and then pulled the car even further over, so that it was completely off the shoulder. He got out of the car and went after her.

She disappeared behind a clump of trees.

"Wren!" he yelled again.

"Go away!" she shrieked back.

"Come on, Wren, what the hell are you doing?"

"I'm taking a motherfucking piss, okay?" she yelled. "Is that okay?"

He stopped moving.

"Go back to the damned car, Reilly," she yelled.

He did. He went back to the car, and he climbed inside, and he shut his eyes, and he thought that he was not going to be able to deal with pregnancy hormones and Wren Delacroix. It was a combination that would be a holy terror unleashed on the world.

He remembered what Janessa had been like, and Janessa

was usually fairly mild tempered. But when pregnant, she would sometimes get so angry that she'd break things and yell. Meek little *Janessa* had been that way. It had gotten worse the more pregnant she'd gotten. He couldn't imagine what Wren would be like.

And this was probably the worst way to be pregnant that he could even think of. It was just... obscene.

He needed to get her off the case. He needed to recuse himself too. This was bullshit, staying on. They couldn't possibly be objective, not about all this. But did it matter?

Say Hawk was guilty. The man had no money to his name. He wasn't going to hire some fancy lawyer who'd make a bunch of sophisticated arguments about the mistakes in the police investigation.

No, it'd probably be a public defender and he'd be cutting some kind of deal, maybe to get out of the death penalty. Although, no. Because there were bodies in West Virginia and Maryland, but none in Virginia, and of the three states in the tri-state covered by the task force, only Virginia had the death penalty.

Huh.

Had that been done by design?

The door to the car banged open and Wren climbed back inside.

She was crying, sucking in noisy breaths and sniffling. She wiped at her eyes with the heel of her hand.

"Hey, Wren," he said. "Hey, are you—"

"Don't." She pushed at him. "Don't, please." She slammed something down on the dashboard.

It was a pregnancy test.

CHAPTER SEVENTEEN

Reilly wasn't sure what to do or say. He didn't think it was appropriate to pick up the pregnancy test and look at it. Anyway, it was kind of gross to do that. Of course, it was also gross for it to be on the dashboard of his car. Should he say something to her about that?

Yeah, um, what would he say?

He started the car and pulled it back on the road.

They drove.

Wren was still sniffling. She was making little hiccuping noises.

"I take it it's positive," Reilly finally said.

"No," said Wren, and her voice broke. "It's negative." She started to sob—loud sobs that shook the interior of the car, as if her heart was broken.

He didn't know what to do or how to respond, and as he was thinking of what to say, she started talking.

"I don't know why I'm crying," she said. "I wanted it to be negative. I'm so relieved that it's negative. It's a good thing."

He reached across the car and seized her hand. He squeezed it.

They drove.

He took her home, and he insisted on letting him walk her inside. She didn't like it, but he wouldn't let her argue with him. He looked around the house, too, because Hawk could be there. Hawk could come looking for her. Reilly made her lock up the place.

"All the windows too," he said. "Make sure they're shut up tight."

"I can handle Hawk if he shows back up."

"If all his murdering has been about you, then it's probably not a great idea," said Reilly.

"I'll be fine. You go now. I'm going to rest."

"Okay," he said. "You're right. It's been a hell of a day for you." He started toward the front door. Then he stopped. "You know, I could stay. What if he shows up or something?"

"I told you, I can handle him."

"Yeah, but I have a gun."

"I need to get a gun," she said.

"Probably wouldn't be a bad idea," he said. "You could get a permit to carry concealed if you wanted."

"Yeah," she said. "Guess it's a good thing you never reported the fact that I killed Kyler Morris."

"You were protecting yourself," said Reilly. "Speaking of which, I still have more sessions I need to make it to with the shrink."

"Well, go do that now, then."

"I can't do it right now," said Reilly.

"If I wasn't so wrecked, I'd say we should go out into the woods and look for Hawk," she said. "But there's no way we'd find him."

"We'll make a plan tomorrow," said Reilly.

"What if he's not in the woods? What if he's halfway to the other side of the country by now?"

"Let's hope that's not the case. It'd be tough to find him then." He hesitated. "You sure you're going to be all right?"

"I'm sure," she said. "Come on, give me some credit, okay? You're acting all weird around me because I cried. I didn't mean to."

"That's not why," he said. "After everything you've been through, anyone would cry."

She laughed a little.

"Okay, okay. I'm leaving." He started towards the door.
"Hey, Reilly?" she said.
"Yeah?"
"Thanks."
"For what?"
"For, you know… dealing with me today."
"You don't have to thank me for that," he said. "We're friends, okay? This is what we do."

* * *

"So, what do you think?" said Reilly, lounging on the couch in Maliah's living room.

"I think that she needs to test again in the morning," said Maliah. " Because those pregnancy tests can give false negatives, especially in the beginning. A girlfriend of mine, she took a test, it was negative, and then she went out and got wasted drunk. Next morning, she tested again. Boom. Positive. The kid turned out okay despite all the drinking she did, though. Luckily. Oh, God, can you imagine Wren Delacroix with a child?"

"Not about that," said Reilly. "I'm sorry I told you about that. I was just reeling from everything today. I mean, about getting Major out of jail for a day pass, like she said. That's crazy, isn't it?"

"It's… unconventional," said Maliah. "It'll probably take a ridiculous amount of paperwork, which I bet you'll want me to file."

"You think we should try it?"

"You obviously want to," said Maliah.

"I don't want to if it's pointless," he said. "Wren wanted me to try."

"Oh, well, if *Wren* wanted you to," said Maliah.

"Hey," he said. "You're not going to be like that about it, are you?"

"Like what?"

"Look, she's been going through a lot, don't you think? So, I just feel like whatever I can do to make it easier for her,

I should do that."

"Do you." She gazed at him evenly.

"What the hell, Maliah?" He threw up his hands.

She just stared at him.

"Okay, do you think we should try to file paperwork to get Major out or not?"

"I think you probably need to talk to Lopez about it," said Maliah. "Because he's the person who'll go to bat for us and make it happen. If he doesn't think that we can do it, then we probably can't."

"Yeah, okay, that makes sense." He nodded. "Probably wait forty minutes or so. Don't want to catch him during dinner. He's pissy when that happens."

"All right," said Maliah. "Since you're here, you want to grab dinner together somewhere? I don't have anything in the house."

"Sure," he said. "Where are you thinking?"

"Let's just go to Billy's," said Maliah. "We can get a beer too. You look like you could use one."

"Ain't that the truth," said Reilly.

* * *

Billy's was primarily a bar, so they didn't have a lot of food, and what they did have was of the non-healthy variety. They served burgers and fries and they also had appetizer stuff like jalapeno poppers.

Reilly and Maliah snagged a table in one of the corners. Billy's wasn't the kind of place with waitresses, however. Reilly found out what Maliah wanted, and then he went up to the counter to order their drinks and their food. He got the beers right away. The food would be brought out to them later.

Reilly went back to the table with the beer, and as he was walking, the door opened, and Wren walked in.

She looked up and saw him and then pointedly looked away. She walked past him, up to the bar.

Reilly went over to the table and set down Maliah's beer.

"You are not going over to talk to her," said Maliah, glaring at him. "Not while I am sitting right here."

"For fuck's sake, Maliah, I need to catch her before she orders something. The last thing she should be doing right now is drinking. She needs to go home and rest."

"I thought you said the test was negative."

"That's not why she shouldn't be drinking. She's been through a lot. She needs to sleep. She needs to be good to herself. Drinking is only going to make her feel worse."

"If you leave me alone at this table and go after another woman, I am getting up and walking out of this bar."

His lips parted. "Jesus, Maliah."

Maliah sighed. "You know what? I'll see you at work tomorrow. Send me a text if you talk to Lopez and he says we should start paperwork for Major."

"Are you kidding me? You're leaving anyway? I'm still here. With you."

She got up out of her seat. She hesitated. Then she sat back down. "You know what? It's not even about her."

"It sounds like it's about her, and there is *nothing*—"

"It's not even about *you*."

"So, then, what? It's about nothing?"

She picked at her thumbnail. "It's like I said before. Maybe we'll never be able to trust each other after the way that we got together. Maybe it's just not possible."

He ran a hand over his chin.

She stood up again. "If you hurry up there, maybe you can cancel my burger before they make it."

"Right." Reilly shoved his hands in his pockets.

"Or maybe you can give it to Delacroix."

"Hey, come on, Maliah."

She shook her head and then picked up her purse. Swinging it over her shoulder, she walked out.

He gazed after her. They'd brought separate cars. Hadn't discussed it, just did it, probably out of force of habit. So, he didn't have to worry about getting home. Still. Maybe he should go after her.

Did she want him to go after her?

He turned back to look at Wren.

He went to her instead. It didn't mean anything, no matter what Maliah wanted to think about it. Hell, maybe it was better this way. He was barely out of his divorce with Janessa. Did he really need to get enmeshed with someone else already? Maybe he and Maliah should call it quits.

Wren looked up at him under hooded eyes. She'd already been drinking at home, he realized. It was the alcohol in her system that had given her the courage to come out in the first place. She was nursing a whiskey on ice. She turned back to it. She sucked liquid through the little stirrer straw in her drink. "What?" she croaked.

"You should be at home," he said.

"You don't get to tell me what to do," said Wren.

He nodded slowly. "Yeah, okay. You're right. You're nobody's business but your own. I'm not trying to order you around. But I think if you get some sleep, you're going to feel better than if you drink the night away."

"It's too early to sleep."

"It's also too early to be as drunk as you are."

She gave him the finger.

He leaned across the bar and asked the bartender to wrap up the food he'd ordered.

"What are you doing, Reilly?" she said.

"Taking you back to your house and making sure you get some food in you."

"Maybe that's not what I want."

"You'll thank me in the morning," he said.

And when the food arrived in takeout boxes, she didn't resist. Maybe it smelled good. Maybe she didn't have as much fight in her as she was trying to make out. She hadn't driven here, so that was a good thing. They got in his car, and went back to her place, and they ate their food at her table in her kitchen.

"You gotta think I'm such an idiot," she said to Reilly.

"I don't think that."

"How could I have fallen for it?" she said.

"You mean Hawk?" said Reilly. "We both did. Everyone did."

"Shouldn't you be with Maliah?" she said.

"Probably," he said.

"Great," muttered Wren. "Like she needs more reasons to hate me."

* * *

"Let me get this straight," Lopez was saying over the phone. "You're telling me that the guy you arrested? The guy who you had all that evidence for? You don't think he did it, and you want me to let you get him out of jail to go on a trip through the woods to look for the guy who you do think did it?"

"Um, yeah," said Reilly. "That's what I'm saying."

"That's insane."

"I kind of thought you might say that," said Reilly. "But I thought maybe if we filled out the right forms and talked to the right people—"

"You can get favors like this when you're riding high and closing cases, sure."

"Well, we did, didn't we? The Adams case, that was probably one of the fastest closed serial cases—"

"Yeah, but if you were wrong, that looks *bad*. And you're admitting you were wrong."

"Well, I mean, the guy confessed," said Reilly. "We thought we were right."

"You're not sure either way, are you? You think maybe it's this Marner guy, but you aren't sure it's not Hill."

"We're not a hundred percent, no."

"So, you want me to release a serial killer into custody—"

"He's probably not a serial killer."

"Probably," said Lopez. He sighed. "I don't even know

why you're coming to me with this. I don't have Major Hill locked up. He's in West Virginia."

"No, I know that, but we thought that if anyone could help us get it done, it would be you. Maliah said I should talk to you first before I tried anything else."

"Here's what I think, Reilly. Try something else. This isn't going to happen. No way, no how."

"Right," muttered Reilly. "Right." He hung up the phone and got out of his car. He'd been having the conversation in the driveway to Maliah's house. He wasn't even sure why he'd driven here. He had done it almost by rote, as if not of his own volition.

He knocked on her door.

She answered it a few moments later, a robe wrapped around her pajamas. "Cai."

"Hey," he said.

"You came by after you tucked her in?"

"I..." He hung his head.

"You got to figure your shit out, Cai."

"There's nothing to figure out," he said. "You're jealous, because I cheated on my wife with you. You don't trust me. It makes sense. But I'm not that kind of a man. I'm not habitual about my infidelity. I never cheated on Janessa before you. I never will again. I've seen how destructive it is and how much pain it causes. Nothing is worth that."

"I want to believe you," she said. "But I just can't."

"Sure, you can. You're not trying."

"No, it's not about trying. It's about something else. Something inside me, something that can't help but feel it. I don't know."

"So, what are you saying?"

"Am I stuttering? Am I speaking in a dialect you don't understand?"

"Are you saying this can't work? Are you saying you want this to be over?"

"Is that what you want?"

"No," he said.

"You sure?'

He threw his hands up in the air. "I don't know why I'm bothering to talk to you about this."

She folded her arms over her chest. "Really? That's your response?"

"I'm going home," he said, turning away from her.

"Yeah, go, sure," she said. "Or go back and check on Delacroix. I'm sure she'd appreciate that."

He turned back around. "Wren is trying to deal with the fact that Hawk is a killer. And I'm trying to be her friend. If there were something more than that going on at this moment, it would be obscene. How can you even think that?"

"Did I say I thought something else was going on?"

"You implied it."

"Did I? Or was that just where your mind was focused, Cai?"

He turned back around. "Forget it. I'm leaving. I can't talk to you right now."

"Sure, go. Run off. That's great," she yelled after him. "That's perfect."

CHAPTER EIGHTEEN

"Morning," said Wren, looking up from the counter at the Daily Bean to see Reilly coming in. She felt like death warmed over, because she'd polished off the rest of a bottle at her place before going out to Billy's. But Reilly had intervened before it got worse, and going to bed after she'd eaten something had helped a lot. She should thank him, but she'd been sentimental enough last night. She wasn't a touchy-feely type. She just waved.

"Morning," said Reilly.

"I ordered your latte," said Wren.

"Yep," chirped Angela from the other side of the counter. "Working on it now."

"Great," said Reilly. He shoved his hands in his pockets. "Uh, how are you doing?"

"Fine," said Wren. "Great. Good. Excellent. Where are we with Major?"

"He's not getting out of jail to show us around in the woods any time soon," said Reilly. "Lopez pretty much shut that down when I floated it past him."

She should have figured. "Yeah, that was a long shot."

"I did, however, get a BOLO set up for Hawk," said Reilly, "but there hasn't been any activity on that. No one's seen him." BOLO stood for 'be on the look-out.'

"That's because he's in the woods," said Wren. "We just need to figure out where."

"Well, maybe we can get together some kind of team to comb the woods. It's a big space out there, but it's not impossible to search. If someone was out there, lost, hurt, we could rally a good search party. In this case, it's someone dangerous, who might hurt someone. Now that he's changed his MO, he could hurt anyone."

"But to rally people, that would involve starting a public panic," said Wren.

"You got a better idea?"

"Let's go talk to Major again," she said.

* * *

"No, I told you," Major said, hands flat on the table in the interrogation room, "I'm not telling you anything. You get me out of here, and I'll show you."

"That's just not possible, Major," said Reilly gently.

"Not possible yet," Wren spoke up. She had been thinking about how she wanted this to go down, and she thought that she could get Major to cooperate if she explained everything to him. "But if you really are innocent—"

"I am," said Major.

"Then you're going to get out, and the best way to do that is to help us find Hawk," said Wren.

"How's that going to help?" said Major. "You think Hawk is going to admit to what he did? Because he's not. He'll blame it on me, or he'll blame it on someone else. Hell, I bet he was blaming that new body you were talking about on someone. Maybe even you."

Wren flinched. Major knew Hawk a little too well.

"Well, listen, you've been arrested," said Reilly. "You're in the system now, and it's not so easy to get you out."

"What we were trying to set up wouldn't have been a release anyway," said Wren. "We were trying to get you, like, a day pass, so that you could come out in the woods with us and show us where the house is."

"That's all?" Major sat back in his chair, looking distraught. "I'm going to go to jail for the rest of my life for this, aren't I? Damn Hawk. I hate that bastard."

"If we find him, you won't," said Wren.

"It won't even matter," muttered Major. "Hawk's too smart. He's got it all figured out."

"Hawk may be smart," said Wren, "but he's got a big liability."

"What's that?" said Major.

"He's compulsive," said Wren.

"Like he can't stop?" said Major.

Wren nodded. "He kept killing after we locked you up, and he couldn't keep himself from following his rituals. If he can't stop, he's going to be caught. And when he does, you're going to go free. Now, come on, Major. Talk to us. Think about how to get to that house."

"But I told you already," said Major. "You have to go out toward where the crazies live."

"What are you talking about, the crazies?" said Wren. "No one lives in those woods."

"They do," said Major.

"Did you see them while you were tripping on acid?" said Reilly flatly.

"They're real!" Major insisted, turning on Reilly.

Wren shot Reilly a look.

Major thought about this for a minute, chewing on his bottom lip. "You know who might now where our house is?"

"Who?" said Wren.

"Roger Green," said Major.

"Roger Green?" said Wren. "He hasn't been back in the compound in years."

"He came by once. We went out to the house in the woods together to do mushrooms."

"When was this?"

"I don't know," said Major. "A few years back. Devon was back with him too, but she said she didn't mess with hallucinogens anymore. Said her mind was plenty open."

"But no one knows where Roger is. He drew a bunch of

weird pictures on the wall of his apartment and split."

"Wait, did we talk to Roger Green?" said Reilly.

Wren nodded at him. "Yeah, we did."

"That place in Baltimore?"

"Yeah."

"He'd be with Devon," said Major.

"He's not with Devon," Wren explained. "They broke up."

"Well, that can't be." Major made a face. "Why does everyone break up? Can't anyone stay together these days?"

Wren rolled her eyes. "Listen, Major—"

"Maybe he would have gone to Cumberland."

"Cumberland?" said Wren. "Cumberland, Maryland?"

"Yeah," said Major. "You remember how David Song talked about that camping ground he stayed at in Cumberland?"

Wren furrowed her brow. "No."

"You have to remember," said Major. "It was this big sermon thing he gave on sanctuary and finding what you needed right when you needed it?"

Wren shook her head.

"He was driving along the interstate," said Major, "and he was on his own. It was before he found the Children. He didn't have anywhere to go. And he prayed to the Lord for help. Immediately, he saw a sign for Hidden Gap Campground."

Wren squinted. " Okay, maybe I kind of vaguely remember this. Did he get there and the car ahead of him paid for his camping fee for the night?"

"Yes!" Major nodded excitedly.

"But what does this have to do with Roger Green?" said Reilly.

"Well, fifteen years ago, after Vivian was arrested, a lot of people fled the compound," said Major. "They didn't have anywhere to go, and they went looking for the campground where David Song had stayed. It was still there.

So, it's a place that people go, members of the Fellowship, anyway. When they need someplace, they go there."

* * *

"Well, I guess we're driving to Cumberland today," said Reilly as they left the jail.

"Yeah, that'll take up the rest of the day for sure," said Wren. "It's a long drive."

"I think it's only maybe an hour and a half," said Reilly. "Two tops." He considered. "But there and back, yeah, it'll be a haul. Not as bad as driving to Richmond, though."

"True," said Wren.

"You think it's possible that Hawk could have gone to this campground?"

"Maybe," said Wren.

"Honestly, it's a long shot that Roger Green's even there," said Reilly. "And say we find him, then what? We ask him to show us where the crazies are in the woods?"

Wren sighed. "You're right, it's stupid. This whole thing is stupid. Maybe we should try to put a team together, like you said, just go combing the woods for Hawk."

Reilly considered, tossing his car keys back and forth in his hands for several minutes. "Well, we don't know where Hawk is, and that house in the woods is our one lead. If this guy can get us out there, we should look for him. But maybe before we drive to Cumberland, we should get in touch with that Devon person, just make sure they haven't made up?"

* * *

"Wren Delacroix?" said Devon's voice over the phone. "I asked you to call me if it turned out that Roger was killing those girls. But you arrested someone else."

"It's not about that," said Wren. "Well, it sort of is, but we don't suspect Roger of anything. We are trying to find him, though."

"I think he's in Cumberland," said Devon.

"You're in touch with him?"

"Well, I wanted to give him the option of knowing his

baby," said Devon. "I felt like it was the right thing to do. I wasn't interested in getting back together with him or anything, but I thought that it wasn't right to keep a father from his son."

"So, it's a boy?" said Wren, smiling. "Congrats."

"Thanks," said Devon. "Yeah, a little boy named Granger."

"How cute," said Wren.

"Anyway, as it turns out, Roger wasn't much interested in the kid," said Devon. "What he was interested in was asking me for money. He gave me an address where I could send it. He's living in some house downtown with a bunch of other losers. I think he's selling drugs." She sighed.

"So, he's not at the Hidden Gap Campground?"

"He was. That's how he ended up in Cumberland. But then he made some friends and moved out. Anyway, I'll give you the address if you want."

"Yeah, thanks," said Wren. "That would be helpful."

* * *

The drive to Cumberland did take nearly two hours. They had to go up to Hagerstown to get on I-70 and take that to I-68. As they drove, they talked about whether or not they thought that Roger was going to want to help them look around in the woods for Hawk, and they determined that he wasn't going to go for it.

But since he'd asked Devon for money, they decided to bribe him.

"We can just promise him money," said Wren.

"What if that's not enough?" said Reilly. "What if he needs to see the cash? I think it's going to be more effective if the money's right there."

"You're not going to give it to him right away, are you?"

"No, not yet. I'll wait until after he takes us to Hawk."

"Well, then, just promise it to him. We don't have cash on us anyway."

"I can go to an ATM," said Reilly. "This is a totally

reimbursable expense. Paying off informants is sometimes necessary. I'll get it out of discretionary funds."

"That's the money you use to pay me, right?" said Wren.

"I don't use *all* of it to pay you," said Reilly.

"Right," said Wren.

When they got off the interstate, they wound through the one-way streets of Cumberland to find an ATM, and then they went looking for Roger. If it hadn't been for the GPS on the phone, they'd both have been lost. The small city had once been a booming place of industry, but all the industry had gone away. The city remained, even if it wasn't bustling or growing these days.

Finally, they reached the address. It was a white house, though the paint was peeling in places, set up on a hill above the street. There were steps up the tiered front lawn, leading to the door.

They climbed and knocked.

A young woman answered the door. She was wearing a shapeless tie-dyed dress and her hair was dyed bright orange. "Yeah?"

"We're looking for Roger Green," said Wren, stepping forward.

"Um… Roger, yeah," said the woman. She stepped aside to let them in. There was a red shag carpet on the floor. It looked as though it had seen better days. The woman leaned back her head and yelled. "Roger!"

"What?" yelled a voice from within.

"You got company," yelled the woman.

A long pause, and then Roger appeared at the top of the steps. He looked them over. "You two."

"Us," said Wren.

"We just want to talk," said Reilly.

"We need your help," said Wren.

"We'll pay," said Reilly.

Roger's eyebrows went up at that. He slowly descended the steps. "Let's talk in the living room." He gestured.

They followed the red carpet into an adjoining room. It did have a couch in it, a sagging black sectional. But that was the only piece of furniture in the room. The walls were bare except for a TV that was mounted to the wall.

None of them sat on the couch.

Roger folded his arms over his chest and surveyed them. "What did you mean, pay?"

"First things first," said Reilly. "Do you remember going back to the compound in Cardinal Falls a few years back and going out into the woods with Major Hill and Hawk Marner?"

"You trying to get me to admit to something?"

"No, we don't care about the mushrooms," said Wren. "We care about the house in the woods. We need to get there. Were you there or not?"

"Yeah, okay, I was there," said Roger. "What's that matter?"

"Could you get us back out there?" said Wren.

Roger thought about this. "Well, it wasn't hard, exactly. There was a path. But finding the path... well, that could be tricky. Besides, I don't want to go back there. That time I went back there and saw Hawk, it wasn't good. Hawk said these things to me... I don't know if I've been right since."

"Well, we'll be with you," said Wren. "Nothing will happen."

"You wouldn't be any match against the things that would try to get me," said Roger.

"Uh, I'm a cop," said Reilly. "Wren has some FBI training. We're not pushovers by any means."

"You can't fight the supernatural," said Roger. "You can't fight the Crimson Ram."

Wren and Reilly exchanged a glance.

"He's stronger out in those woods," said Roger. "And with those murders of those girls, what you were talking to me about before? Sacrifices to him, I bet. He's even stronger."

"You'll be safe," said Reilly. "We won't be alone."

"We won't?" said Wren.

"We'll bring some uniforms," said Reilly.

"Oh, I guess we would do that," said Wren.

"I don't know," said Roger.

"We'll pay," said Reilly again. He got the money out of his pocket. Counted it.

Roger swallowed. "You'd give all that?"

Reilly nodded. " Absolutely. As soon as we get to that house in the woods, it's all yours."

Roger lifted his chin. "Okay, then."

CHAPTER NINETEEN

"What was that?" said Officer Anderson.
" Something in the woods, " said Wren. " Could be anything. Could be an animal. Could be the wind."
"Could be Hawk Marner," said Anderson.
Wren and Reilly were out in the woods the following day with two backup uniforms, who Wren only knew as Anderson and Miller, and with Roger Green, who wasn't taking well to being in the woods.
"It's probably him," breathed Roger. He was in the lead, because he was supposed to be showing them the way through the woods, but he was pretty timid. He'd stopped several times already, not due to noises, but due to things he "felt" in the air that freaked him out. Only the promise of the money drove him onward.
"That's what I think," said Anderson.
"He doesn't mean him, like Hawk him," said Wren.
"What's he mean then?" said Miller.
"Oh, you know," said Reilly. "He means a great horned creepy god that wants sacrifices and stuff."
"I'm checking it out," said Anderson.
"Fine," said Reilly. "Probably a good idea."
Anderson took off in the direction of the sound, wading through the undergrowth in the woods. Most of the trees had lost their leaves at this point, and the undergrowth was dying off for the autumn too, so there wasn't too much to wade through. Even still, it wasn't long before the forest swallowed him up, and they couldn't see him anymore.

They weren't on any kind of discernible path, at least not that Wren could see. This was a part of the woods that Wren had never been in. It was up near the northern part of the compound, back behind the meeting house. The spot where the girls had been killed had been in the south, near the fire pit. She wasn't familiar with any part of the forest at all, though.

She'd never played out here as a kid. None of them had. When they were away from the compound, out near their schools, forests seemed like exciting adventure-filled places to explore. But here, this forest… it was different. Something about it made her feel cold all over.

She didn't much like being in here now, and she wasn't too confident that Roger was going to be able to lead them anywhere. He wanted that money pretty bad. He could easily be only pretending to know where the house was.

Sure, Reilly had told him he wouldn't get the money until he showed them where the house was, but Reilly also had the money on him. He'd shown it to Roger. So, it was possible that Roger might attack Reilly, go for the money. It could be bad.

Wren needed to keep an eye on Roger, make sure he didn't try anything.

Right then, Roger was looking around, turning in a tight circle, glancing every which way, as if he thought that he'd be attacked at any moment himself. Maybe he wasn't anything to worry about after all.

"What the hell?" Reilly said. "What's keeping Anderson?"

"Maybe it's the crazies," said Roger quietly.

"What?" said Wren, turning on him. "What about the crazies?"

"They live around here," said Roger. "They used to be one with us, but they were overtaken by the Horned Lord. He took their sanity, and he forced them to live like beasts."

"Um? One with us?" said Wren.

"In the Fellowship," said Roger. "They used to be Vivian's favorites. But then they betrayed her. They betrayed the Horned Lord."

Reilly raised his voice. "Anderson? You find anything?"

There was no response.

Except Wren felt as though the wind picked up deliberately, blowing the dry, dead leaves up from the ground. The fingers of the breeze came for her, penetrating her clothes, clawing at the back of her neck. In spite of herself, she shivered.

"I fucking hate it in these woods," she muttered.

Miller spoke up. "We should have brought walkies." The uniforms always had walkie-talkies, but they were anchored to the radios in their cars. They'd decided to ditch them because they'd be too deep in the woods to talk to dispatch.

"To talk to each other," said Reilly. "Right. That would have been smart. But we, apparently, are idiots." He bowed his head, and spoke more to himself that anyone else, "Sure, let's go into the woods with a guide who's afraid of a scary antlered god. Sure, let's split up when we hear a strange noise." He raised his gaze to look at them. "All right, after Anderson, all of us together. This isn't turning into *The Hills Have Eyes* on my watch."

"Oh, fuck no," said Miller. "You ever notice how cops always get killed first in those kinds of movies?"

"I have," said Reilly, giving him a grim smile. He stalked off into the woods.

Wren started after him.

"That's not the way," said Roger.

"We have to get Anderson," said Reilly.

"That's *not* the way." Roger's voice was getting shrill.

"Um..." Wren stopped. "Maybe we should listen to him."

"We're not splitting up," Reilly called back. "And we need to get to Anderson. Come on."

"I'm starting to wonder if these crazies aren't exactly

hallucinations," Wren called.

"Yeah?" said Reilly. "You think?"

"So, it's probably not a good idea to go over there."

Reilly stopped walking and turned to face her. " You want to leave Anderson to these crazies?"

She sighed. She turned to Roger. "Come on, Roger."

"No," said Roger.

"Reilly's got a gun," said Wren. "Miller's got a gun. And we can shoot the crazies, can't we?"

"We can," said Roger. " But we can't be sure that the Horned Lord won't raise them back up and force them to keep doing his bidding."

She grabbed Roger by the arm. "Come on."

* * *

After walking for several minutes, they emerged into a clearing. It was small, and it had obviously been cleared out manually, because there were tree trunks everywhere.

In the middle of the clearing was a wooden structure, like a framed-out pavilion with no roof. The center came to a point above and there was a pole in the middle. Inside the pavilion was a round table. Or maybe an altar. It was fitted together from stone, but the stone was stained dark, almost black. It could have been stained with blood.

They all stopped and gaped at it.

" Okay, who made that?" said Reilly. " Did Hawk and Major make that?"

"The crazies made that," said Roger.

"Karen and Terrence Freeman," said Wren in a soft voice. "It's them, isn't it? They're the ones who betrayed Vivian."

"The people who turned her in?" said Reilly. "You think they're out in the woods?"

"I thought they were dead," said Wren. "No one's heard from them in years. But I'm right, aren't I?" She turned to Roger. "It's them. They're the crazies?"

Roger nodded. " The Horned Lord took their sanity as punishment."

Miller pointed at the pavilion. "Look, no crazy person built that. That's very deliberate." He started towards it.

"Hey, wait up," said Reilly, hurrying after him.

Wren hesitated.

"Delacroix, come on," Reilly said.

Wren tugged on Roger's arm. He resisted for a minute, but then he came along with her.

Closer to the pavilion, they could see that there were piles of bones around the foot of it. The bones could have been animal bones, like the stacks on the stone circle where the girls had been killed, but Wren didn't think so. They looked human to her.

Yes. There was a human skull.

But as much as she wanted to stop, something drove her forward. It was that curiosity within her, that perverse fascination with death. Maybe it wasinherited from Vivian. Maybe it coursed through her veins, her birthright. She yanked Roger along with her and they grew closer still.

Now, Wren could see that the middle post of the pavilion was carved in the shape of the Crimson Ram. He stood upright, gazing down at the altar beneath him, and his face was terrible. Red stains splashed against him, splashed down on the wooden floor of the pavilion, splashed against the posts that held it up. And closer now, she could smell the stench of death.

Things were killed here.

People were killed here.

They were slaughtered.

What was this place?

CHAPTER TWENTY

Reilly put a hand on Wren's shoulder.
She jumped, as if startled out of a pleasant reverie. She was standing at the mouth of the pavilion, staring inside, transfixed. Now, she turned to him, almost guiltily. "Yeah?"
"This is something," said Reilly. "I don't know if you're right, if it's those Freeman people, and if they're living out here in the woods, like, killing people or something, but... well, this is a crime scene. We need to report this."
"Definitely," said Wren, nodding. "Yeah, this is something big. It's ritualistic. Whoever does this follows a series of very set steps. There is a definite psychosis here, but it's highly functional. I don't know if it's just Terrence, or if Karen helps. Even if she doesn't, she must be complicit."
"The question is," said Reilly, "should we call it in now, or just take note and keep going? Because if we bring a bunch of police officers into the woods—"
"Then Hawk will get spooked and leave," said Wren.
"Exactly," said Reilly. "Assuming he's out here, this is our best chance to find him."
"Yeah," she said. "It is. We can't report this yet."
"That's what I'm thinking," he said. He got out his phone.
"You have service?" she said.
"Uh..." He looked. "It looks like it's going in and out. But that isn't what I wanted to do. I have an app on here that will do the latitude and longitude. We need to note that so we can get back out here and bring a team."

"Oh, smart," said Wren. "I should get an app like that. Sounds cool."

"It is." He scrolled through his screen. He pulled up the app and let it do its thing. Once the coordinates were stored, he named and saved them.

"What about Anderson?" said Miller.

"What about him?" said Reilly.

" Well, it's obvious that whoever's out here is dangerous," said Miller. "I'd say there's a ninety percent chance they've got Anderson. And what are you saying? We just leave him and go on after Hawk Marner?"

"No," said Reilly, shaking his head. "No, look, we're here looking for Anderson. We're going to find him. And then we get back on track to going to that house. Right, Roger?"

Roger was sitting on the grass, his back to the pavilion. He was muttering to himself.

"Roger?" called Reilly.

Roger got up and trudged over to them. "I never should have come out here with you two. I knew this was a bad idea. I could feel it. We have to stay *away* from the crazies."

"All right," said Reilly. "So, assuming Anderson got to this clearing, then where would he have gone after this?"

"There," said Wren, pointing. "That look like a path to you?"

"It does," said Reilly.

They left the pavilion and crossed the clearing to the opening of the path. It was narrow, but well-worn. They went single file back into the woods. Reilly went first, then Miller, then Roger. Wren brought up the rear, and she thought to herself, as they walked, that it was a particularly stupid way for them to be walking. Someone armed should be bringing up the rear.

She needed to get a gun.

Once she got out of here, she was going to do that. She was going to look into one of those concealed carry licenses too.

They weren't walking long before they came to a cabin. It was nestled in the woods, and it looked a lot like one of the cabins that had been built on the compound. It had windows and doorknobs and all sorts of things that couldn't be sourced from the woods. Whoever had built this would have had access to materials at the compound.

They paused outside, waiting for someone to come out of the cabin, someone to notice they were there.

But everything was still.

The only sound was a distant chirping bird, somewhere off in the forest.

Reilly looked at Roger. "Is this it? Is this Hawk's cabin?"

"No," said Roger.

"Major said that it was primitive," said Wren. "No glass for the windows or anything. This has glass."

"Right," said Reilly. He shot Wren a glance and then he headed for the cabin.

They followed him.

They tried the front door and found it unlocked. They stepped inside.

It was set up like the cabins on the compound, living room on the right, kitchen on the left just when they came in. The living room had a couch and a woven rug on the wooden floor. The kitchen didn't have modern appliances. There was a two-basin sink set into the counter, but no faucet. A wood stove was set into the divide between the kitchen and living room, obviously used for cooking and for heating.

There were dishes in the sink and a bucket of water sitting on the counter next to them.

Someone had been in the cabin recently.

They looked through the rest of the place. Two bedrooms, one with a full-sized bed and another with two twin-sized beds, both covered in patchwork quilts that looked hand sewn. But no one else was inside the cabin.

They went out a back door, at the end of the hallway between the bedrooms.

Behind the house, there were two other buildings. One was far off, small, obviously an outhouse. The second looked like some kind of outdoor kitchen, maybe used in the summer when it was too hot to cook in the main house.

Between both of them was Officer Anderson, hanging upside down from a tree branch, his ankles lashed to the tree. His throat had been cut, and his blood was dripping down over his face into a bucket.

CHAPTER TWENTY-ONE

Roger screamed.

Reilly tackled him, mashing his hand over the man's mouth. "Shut up," he said fiercely. "Shut up."

Miller was white-faced, shaking. He stalked to Anderson, yanking a pocket knife out. He trembled as he managed to get the blade out and cut Anderson down. Gently, he lay the other man out on the ground. He bent down next to him and checked for his pulse. At his neck, at his wrist.

Reilly let go of Roger. "Shh."

Roger nodded. There was no blood in his lips.

Reilly took out his phone. "I don't have any service."

"You had service near the pavilion, right?" said Wren, who knew that the game had changed now. A dead man meant that they called this in. There was no way that they could keep pushing on for Hawk, not after this.

"Yeah," said Reilly. "Okay, I'm going to head back there—"

"You're the one who said we shouldn't split up," said Miller, who was still staring down at Anderson. His voice wasn't strong.

"Well, someone should stay with the body," said Reilly. "Probably more than one someone. You stay here with Roger, and Delacroix and I will—"

"We'll bring Anderson with us." Miller still wasn't looking at Reilly.

"That's not good," said Wren. "We move him from the scene, we'll screw up the evidence."

"Whoever did this is out there," said Miller, finally raising his head. "We can't leave him here, and we can't stay. We have to get out of here. We're in danger. We'll drag him out. If we all help, we can do it."

"Come on, Miller," said Reilly. "Get up, draw your weapon."

Miller looked back at Anderson.

"Now," Reilly growled.

Miller swallowed hard. He got to his feet and unholstered his gun.

Reilly took his out too.

They both disengaged their safeties.

"You ever discharged your weapon in the line of duty?" said Reilly to Miller.

Miller didn't answer.

"You'll be fine," said Reilly. "Now, I'm going to go and call this in, and I'll be right back." He nodded at Roger. "You stay here with Miller, okay?"

Roger shook his head. "No," he said. "I'm getting out of here." He scrambled to his feet and dove off into the woods, running between the trees.

Reilly opened his mouth as if to call after him. Then he thought better of it. Closed his mouth. Glanced at Wren. "Damn it."

"You want me to go after him?" she said.

"Stay with Miller," said Reilly. He headed around the house.

Wren watched him go.

Behind her, a grunt.

She whirled.

There was someone behind Miller. A figure. A man. He was wearing dirty, patched clothes, and he had a full beard and long hair.

Miller twisted, pulling the trigger on his pistol.

Loud bangs echoed through the forest.

Reilly yelled.

Wren twisted to see him coming back.

"Down, Wren!" he shouted.

She hit the ground.

All she could hear was gunfire.

She was face down on the ground. She twisted to try to see what was going on. Miller was lying face down on the ground, too. There was a knife his back, the hilt still sticking out. Miller wasn't moving.

The bearded man was behind him, on one knee, clutching his shoulder. He was bleeding. He must have been shot.

But then Wren realized that Reilly wasn't shooting anymore. Shouldn't he shoot the bearded man again? The man was obviously dangerous. He posed a threat.

She craned her neck around to see Reilly.

Except Reilly was on the ground too, and there was someone on top of him, a figure dressed in patched clothes, but this one was a woman. She brought another knife down into Reilly's chest, sticking him over and over again.

CHAPTER TWENTY-TWO

Wren shrieked. She scrambled to her feet, but then she hesitated. She had been intending to go for the woman, knock him off Reilly, but maybe she should get Miller's gun.

She turned to look at him. Where was it? He'd been holding it, but he wasn't holding it now. If he'd dropped it—

Damn it, what about Reilly?

She turned back and hurled herself at the woman on top of him.

They struggled on the ground together. The woman got over Wren and tried to push the knife into Wren's skin. Wren grabbed the woman's wrist and held the tip of the knife just far enough away.

They both grunted, evenly matched as far as strength.

"Not the girl," said the man's voice. He sounded as though he was in pain.

"That's right," hissed the woman. "He wanted you alive."

"Who wanted me alive?" said Wren. "Hawk? Is it Hawk? Have you seen Hawk?"

The woman threw her head back and then slammed her forehead into Wren's nose.

Wren screamed in pain. Blood gushed out of her nose.

The woman stood up and kicked her over, back on her stomach. Wren felt the woman gather her wrists together. She was being tied up.

She struggled, but she didn't manage to get away. Her hands were tied. She looked at Reilly, who was motionless on the ground, his eyes closed, his shirt turning bright red. She thought about how she didn't usually see him in casual clothes, hiking clothes, how he was usually wearing a suit, and she thought that he looked good in a t-shirt. Or he had, anyway, before he'd been stabbed.

The woman wrenched Wren from behind, forcing Wren to her feet.

Now, the man was getting to his feet. He came over to her, lifting her chin. "You're all grown up."

"It *is* you," said Wren, recognizing him. "Terrence Freeman. You're not dead after all."

"You were just a little thing when it happened," said Terrence.

"Doesn't matter," said the woman. "We have her, now what do we do? Do we take her to him?"

"No, you know we have to do the sacrifice first."

"But what if he hurts them before we're finished?"

"If we go to him without the skin of the black man, he'll kill them. You heard him say that," said Terrence. "Karen, please, get the knives and prepare. I'll tie Wren up in the house."

"Skin?" said Wren. "The skin?"

"Quiet," said Terrence. He forced Wren back into the cabin.

"Listen," said Wren, "if Hawk is threatening you, you should let me free. Let me talk to him. Whatever he's doing, trust me, I'm the best person to talk him out of it."

"We can't take any risks," said Terrence. "I'm sorry about your friend." He brought her into the living room of the house and stretched her arms up. He tied them to a hook in the ceiling. The ceiling wasn't that high in the cabin.

Wren struggled, but she couldn't get free. This was going to be hell in five minutes. She was going to lose all the blood in her hands. "Please, Terrence," she said. "Let me go. Is it Hawk? Can you at least tell me that?"

Terrence walked out of the cabin.

"Hey!" yelled Wren after him, trying to kick out her legs, to touch the walls or the furniture or something. She couldn't.

***

Reilly was going in and out of consciousness. When he'd been tackled by that woman, he'd hit his head on a rock. He was pretty sure he had a concussion. His head was pounding in a painful way—the kind of pain he'd never even really knew existed. Nothing in his life had ever hurt him this bad.

Other things hurt too, but not as much.

He was being dragged over the ground, and whenever they went over a stone or a bump, it made everything hurt worse. His head, his chest...

Oh, fuck, he'd been stabbed, hadn't he? He was bleeding. He was bleeding a lot. He was pretty sure the blood loss wasn't really helping with his consciousness. But, well, they seemed to have missed anything vital, whoever had done the stabbing. His heart was still beating. His lungs weren't punctured.

Always something to be grateful for, as his grandmother would say.

He wasn't sure why he was thinking that, not in this moment. It was a stupid time to be practicing gratitude. No, now was the time for action. Of course, he was tied up. His arms were tied above his head. They were being dragged behind him. Someone had him by the feet, which were also tied. That was how he was being dragged.

Gun, he thought. *Where's my gun?*

Gone, of course. Whoever had done this to him wouldn't have tucked his pistol back into its holster or anything like that.

He groaned. He didn't mean to. It just came out of his mouth.

The dragging continued. He was dragged out of the woods and back into the clearing, back to the pavilion. He could see the man that was dragging him had a ponytail. Long, dark hair. And a beard. He remembered that from when the guy was stabbing Miller.

Was Miller all right? Hell, if he started getting uniforms killed, it was going to be harder than ever to get people to volunteer for the task force.

Of course, Reilly was pretty sure that being dragged onto this pavilion was a bad sign in terms of his own life expectancy.

The man—Terrence Freeman, right?—hoisted Reilly up onto the altar in the center. He was strong. Terrence wrapped Reilly around the center post, tying his arms and his legs together, painfully bending Reilly's back.

Reilly let out another grunting noise.

"Sorry about this," said Terrence. "It's not a racial thing, I swear. I got nothing against black people."

Reilly glared at the man. "Yeah? Really?"

"Sure," said Terrence. "It's not even personal. We catch what we can out here. We have a mandate. Got to sacrifice the ones we do. We tried to get out of it before. You can't run from God, though."

"God," Reilly repeated. "Sure. You're doing God's work."

"He works in mysterious ways," said Terrence. "Race isn't anything to him. God is no respecter of persons. He doesn't care if you're black or white or purple. If he decrees it's your time, then it's your time. And I am only a servant in his master plan."

"Which he communicates to you how?" Reilly didn't know what he was doing. Did he really think he could argue this man out of his crazy faith? Obviously, the guy was committed. And not only that, experienced. No, going at this rationally, it was exactly the wrong call. The more he argued, the more the man would shore up his walls until he became impenetrable. He needed a different plan.

"Well, in various ways." Terrence unrolled a roll of

fabric. Inside were three very sharp knives.

Reilly grimaced. "You don't want to do this."

"You're right," said Terrence. "I don't. It's the Lord that wants it. He makes the commands, and I follow through. I figure this is punishment for a few months back, when we let one go. We saw him out in the woods, walking past us, and we didn't take him. None of us takes any pleasure in it, you know. It's a messy and awful business, back-breaking too. I'd be happy enough to never have to kill another man."

"Then don't," said Reilly.

"Got to," said Terrence, selecting one of the knives. He peered down at Reilly. "I have to say, though, I've never carved up a black man. All that dark skin of yours… it's exotic."

Exotic? Seriously? Reilly gazed up at the top of the pavilion, seething. This was not the way he died. Not at the hands of this idiotic backwoods man who thought his skin was exotic. No, he was getting out of here, and he had to be smart.

Terrence ran his finger over the blade of the knife, testing it. "So, I'll cling to that novelty to help me through it. I expect it'll all be the same once we get skin deep. I had this friend named LaShawn once, back when I was in college." He set down the knife and selected another one. "Bet you never thought I went to college, did you?"

"I didn't say that," said Reilly, even though he had painted an idea of the man as ignorant in his mind. Knowing that he wasn't, it made Reilly hate him even more. It made what he was doing even more evil.

"Well, I did," said Terrence. "Didn't graduate. One summer, I ended up out at the compound, and I listened to the words of David Song and I tripped on acid with Vivian Delacroix, and I never did leave after that. Tried to, but I couldn't. The Lord wasn't pleased that I didn't want to do his bidding." He tested the second knife. "Anyway, LaShawn. He and I used to play basketball one-on-one at

148

one of the hoops on campus. He'd always trounce me, and I used to say it was on account of his being black. Because, I mean, everyone knows black people are better at basketball."

Reilly gritted his teeth. If there was any fairness in the universe, right now, he'd be able to snap the ropes binding him and use them to strangle Terrence. But life wasn't fair. Actually, his grandmother had been fond of saying that too.

Terrence began matter-of-factly slicing through the sleeve of Reilly's t-shirt. "But he told me I was worthless, racist sack of shit for saying that."

Reilly swallowed. "Did he?"

"Well, I didn't know any better," said Terrence. "I thought it was science. I thought they'd proved it and black men had more blood vessels or something. LaShawn said that it was all social. That when a boy grows up in a world where the only kind of powerful men like him that he sees are basketball stars and rappers, he gets the idea that he better get good at one of those things. He said there was no difference between black men and white men, no advantage that made black men better than white men at basketball. He said it was just a sign that we lived in a racist cesspool of a world, and that I was lucky to have been born white." He sliced through the front of Reilly's shirt and then cut off the other sleeve.

The ribbons of Reilly's shirt fell to the floor of the pavilion.

"I saw things different after that," said Terrence. "I guess I'd never really put myself in a black man's place before. I'd never thought of what it would be like." He surveyed Reilly. "I'm not sure why I'm telling you this."

"I'm not sure either," said Reilly, looking up at him. Deep down, he knew that his best strategy for getting mercy was to be vulnerable, expose his weaknesses, and beg for this man not to hurt him. But he was goddamned if he thought he could do that right now. Beg from this guy? Oh, hell, no.

"I'd kill you before I skinned you," said Terrence apologetically. "But I have to spill blood on the altar. It's what the Lord decrees. I'm afraid this is going to really hurt."

Reilly struggled against the ropes that held him again, knowing it was useless, but not being able to stop himself. But nothing happened. The ropes dug painfully into his wrists and ankles, and he couldn't get anywhere.

Terrence ran the blade of the knife over Reilly's chest, not cutting him, just testing it out, marking his path.

Reilly shivered in spite of himself.

"For the glory of the Crimson Ram," Terrence breathed, and then his blade bit into Reilly's skin.

CHAPTER TWENTY-THREE

Wren was trying to slip her hands out of the ropes that held her to the ceiling, but she wasn't having a lot of luck. They were tied too tightly, and she had long since lost much feeling in her hands or fingers. They were bloodless and pale above her and she could only feel pins and needles.

Karen Freeman was kneeling down, putting fire into the wood stove.

"Karen," said Wren. "You don't have to do this. Let me down. Let's talk about this."

Karen ignored her. She went back into the kitchen part of the house and got out a very large cast iron pot. It was really more like a cauldron, like something a witch would have and use to boil things over the fire. She set the cauldron on top of the wood stove.

"Hawk's the person threatening you, isn't he?" said Wren. "Can you at least tell me that?"

Karen went back into the kitchen and got three empty buckets. She went out the front door.

Leaving Wren alone.

Wren looked around, trying to see how she could use this sudden lack of supervision to her advantage. But she couldn't, not unless she could get her hands free.

She tried kicking out her legs, but the strain on her wrists was agonizing, and she couldn't reach anything anyway.

A cry of frustration escaped her lips.

Karen was back, lugging three buckets of water. She set them down in front of the wood stove.

"I know Hawk. I understand him," said Wren. "I know that I can convince him not to do whatever he's threatened to do. Who has he threatened? Who is he trying to hurt?"

Karen picked up one of the buckets and carefully poured the water into the cauldron.

"Okay, what are you doing with that?" said Wren. "Something tells me you're not making soup."

Karen turned to her, a dull look in her eyes. "We do what we must."

Wren's voice broke. "Is that for Reilly? Those bones I saw piled around the pavilion out there, they were pretty clean. You boil them, don't you?"

Karen picked up the next bucket and poured it into the cauldron.

"You don't have to hurt Reilly," said Wren. "Um, Caius. His name is Caius. He's a good man. He has a son named Timmy. Timmy's autistic, and he's just learning to talk, even though he's ten years old. Reilly—Caius. He and his wife, they found this way to reach the kid, and if you kill Reilly now, before he has the chance to hear his son talk, that would be the cruelest thing I could possibly think of. I remember you, Karen. You're not cruel. You're a good woman. You turned in my mother. You stopped the murders. You and Terrence did the right thing. How could you be out here murdering people?"

Karen dumped in the third bucket, but she wasn't as careful. Water splashed out on the floor. "Damn," said Karen, going to get a rag. She got down on her hands and knees.

"Let Reilly go, and we'll help you get Hawk," said Wren. "I know he threatened to kill someone, but we'll stop him."

Karen wiped up the water. "We can't risk that, Wren. I'm sorry."

Oh, God. Karen was talking back.

"You can," said Wren. "You're a good person. I know you are. You don't have to do this."

152

Karen looked up at her, and her eyes were shining. "We wanted to be good, but it was too late."

"It's never too late."

"We are consecrated to the Horned Lord," said Karen. "We gave ourselves to him to do his bidding, whether for good or for evil."

"The Crimson Ram isn't evil. David Song said—"

"He's both," said Karen. "The Lord is the source of all the good in the world, but also the source of all the evil. There must be evil, Wren, because without it, there would be no good. There must be balance. We pledged ourselves to him, and then we tried to take it back. We turned in Vivian, and she was arrested, and the work of the Lord was stopped. He needed it to continue. He forced us to come out here and exile ourselves. And we have to kill. And because we were not satisfied to do as he asked before, because we tried to take it all into our own hands, we must do the worst thing we can imagine. We must kill and eat others."

"Eat?" said Wren.

Karen's face crumpled. "It is our punishment, Wren, to be as beasts."

"Look, this is bullshit." Wren shook at the ropes hanging her from the ceiling. "Who told you this?"

"We saw it in a vision," said Karen.

"So... Terrence?" said Wren. "He told you?"

"It came from the Lord," said Karen.

"There's no Horned Lord," said Wren. "He's made up. He's not real. All this, out here, you don't have to do any of it."

"I wish he was made up," said Karen. "Oh, how I wish it. When Terrence and I went to the police, I thought that we could escape him. I thought we gave him the power, our allegiance was what made him strong. I thought if we took our belief back, he would be weak. But..." She sat back on her knees and wiped at her eyes. "That's not what happened."

"Okay, look, not Reilly," said Wren. "You have to help me with Reilly. You can sacrifice someone else."

"Hawk wants the black man dead," said Karen.

"Well, screw Hawk," said Wren. "I'm telling you, I can handle Hawk."

"Hawk is in communication with the Lord," said Karen. "He and the Lord speak together, and Hawk is his servant as much as we are. Hawk must kill as well. If the Crimson Ram has decided he wants more sacrifice from us, he will use Hawk to extract it from us. This is not the time to be weak. We have to do as we are commanded."

"No," said Wren. "No, please. Reilly's a good man, I'm telling you. You can't take him away from his son. He's a father—"

"Shut up," said Karen, getting to her feet. "Just *shut up*."

"I won't," said Wren. "I refuse to be quiet if you're just standing by while an innocent man is slaughtered."

Karen threw back her head and let out an ear-piercing shriek.

***

The scream cut through the air and Terrence looked up from what he was doing to Reilly.

Reilly panted. He should be screaming like that. There was a T shape cut into his chest. Shallow cuts, not that deep, but Terrence had been starting to peel back the skin under Reilly's collarbone, and Reilly had been thrashing away from him, but not making any noise, gritting his teeth, biting the inside of his cheek, but not making a sound, because…

Well, hell, he didn't know why.

Now, though, this scream, and Terrence stopped.

Blood dripped down Reilly's chest, down onto stone surface of the altar where Reilly was tied up. It made a plopping noise, like a leaky faucet.

Terrence raised his hand, still holding his bloody knife, shading his eyes as he looked in the direction of the cabin. He raised his voice. "Karen?"

Seconds ticked by. There was no sound except the drip of Reilly's blood.

Reilly made a funny gasping noise, his breath catching in his throat.

"Karen!" yelled Terrence. "What's wrong?"

No response from Karen.

Terrence looked back at Reilly. "That woman, I swear."

Reilly licked his lips. "Better go check on her."

Terrence raised his eyebrows at him. " You concerned about my wife? Somehow I highly doubt that."

"She alone?"

"Well, Wren's with her."

"No telling what Wren did to her," said Reilly, baring his teeth.

"Oh, come on. Little Wren Delacroix? I remember her as a little girl. She was so sweet."

"Well, she's grown up now," said Reilly. "She takes after her mother. She's got a vicious streak."

Terrence ' s face twitched. He scratched his forehead, leaving behind a streak of Reilly's blood. " Well, hell, " he muttered. He stabbed the knife into one of the posts of the pavilion. The hilt was several inches from Reilly ' s face. " Don ' t go anywhere, huh? " Terrence chuckled, and then walked off, leaving Reilly alone.

Reilly looked at the knife, sticking out there, taunting him. He listened to his blood dripping against the stone altar beneath him. He leaned his head back so that he could see where Terrence was, and he waited until the man was across the field, almost into the woods.

Then Reilly started to move. He had an idea. It probably wouldn't work, but he had to try something.

If he managed to wriggle all the way around this post here in the middle, he could line up his arms and legs with that knife. Maybe he could manage to get the rope over there, to use the knife to saw through it. Maybe he could get free.

He shifted his hips, moving the muscles in his stomach

to inch around.

Blood spurted out of his wounds.

He grunted.

But he'd moved. Only a little, sure, but it was something. He didn't know how much time he'd have until Terrence came back. He had to keep trying.

And so, he did.

Blood gushed against the altar.

Reilly cried out in pain.

CHAPTER TWENTY-FOUR

Karen was stuffing the rag she'd used to clean the floor into Wren's mouth.

Well, she was trying. She wasn't succeeding, because Wren was kicking her.

Terrence appeared in the doorway. "What the hell are you doing up here?"

Karen turned on him, shaking the rag at him. "She won't keep her mouth shut. She's driving me out of my mind."

"Ignore her," said Terrence. "This is why you're screaming bloody murder? Because she's *talking*? I thought you were being stabbed to death the way you were screaming."

Karen glared at him. "I don't like any of this, Terrence. I *hate* it. It makes me ill what we do out here. Are we sure it's the will of the Lord?"

"We let that one go, Karen, and now this," said Terrence. "You know this is what comes of getting soft."

"Well, at least the girls aren't here to see this one," said Karen, going back into the kitchen. She flung the rag down on the counter.

"Girls?" said Wren.

"Shut up," said Karen, pointing at her. She turned back to Terrence. "Can't we knock her out or something?"

"Do what you want, just don't kill her," said Terrence, turning his back on her.

"What girls?" said Wren, who wasn't having too much trouble putting this together. The other room with the two beds? "You have daughters? Does Hawk have your daughters? How old are they?"

Karen's eyes snapped to Wren's, holding her gaze. "How do you know that?"

"Not hard to figure out," said Wren. "Are they young?"

"They're twins," said Karen. "They're eleven."

"Oh, no," said Wren.

"Just how he likes them," said Karen, her voice cracking. "If we don't do *exactly* as he says, he'll hurt our little girls. He'll take them from us." Tears were starting to spill out of her eyes. "Hell, he might do it anyway if we don't hurry."

"Take me to him," said Wren. "Take me now. It's not about the girls, it's about me. He kills them because he wants *me*. Let Reilly go, and I'll save your daughters, I swear."

Karen turned to Terrence, questions in her eyes.

"I was that age," said Wren. "Remember? I was that age when Hawk and I were paired. It's all about me, don't you see? If you let me go to him, I can stop all of this."

"Karen," said Terrence, shaking his head. "You gotta stop listening to her. This isn't about Hawk, it's about our duty to the Lord."

"But do we really have a duty?" she said. "Maybe we just are looking at it a certain way, and maybe—"

"Come with me," said Terrence, taking her by the arm. "Leave her here and bear witness while I fulfill the sacrifice."

"But if she could talk to Hawk," said Karen. "Maybe then this could all stop."

"No," said Terrence, yanking on her arm. He dragged her out of the cabin.

* * *

Terrence dragged Karen along after him until they got back to the pavilion. He looked over Reilly, but the man was just as he'd left him, except there was a good bit more blood on the altar than there had been.

"Stand here," he told Karen. "You need to watch."

Karen was openly sobbing, and not bothering to brush her tears away. "I just want our babies back. That's all I want. I don't want to kill. I never wanted this."

"I tell you the truth," said Terrence in an imperious voice. " Unless you eat of the flesh, you have no life in you. Whoever eats of the flesh will have eternal life, and will be raised up on the last day."

"But Terrence—"

" Verily, verily, the skin must be taken and the blood spilled and the flesh consumed," roared Terrence. Then he squinted. "Now, where the hell did I put that knife?"

"Right here," said Reilly, springing up off the altar. He buried the knife in Terrence's stomach.

Terrence bent over, letting out a grunt.

Reilly pulled the knife out.

Terrence grabbed for Reilly with one hand, groping. The other hand went to the wound in his stomach.

Reilly punched the knife into the man's chest. Blood gushed out, onto Reilly's hands. The knife handle was slippery.

"No!" Karen screamed. She hurled herself at Reilly.

Reilly staggered backwards.

Karen caught Terrence.

He turned his head at her. His eyes were dull. He tried to say something, but only gurgling noises came out of his throat.

Karen sobbed. "No, no, no."

Reilly backed up until he collided with one of the pavilion posts. He pointed the knife at Karen.

She looked up at Reilly and down at Terrence, and then she got up and took off running into the woods.

Reilly pushed off the pavilion and went after her. She was going back to the cabin, and Wren was there.

But Reilly couldn't go quickly, and Karen was running. He lost sight of her almost immediately.

When he finally reached the cabin, he opened the door. Steam rolled out, billows of it.

He coughed. What the hell? Then he realized there was a pot on the stove, water boiling. He spied Wren in the living room, tied to the ceiling. He staggered over to her and cut her down.

"Reilly," she said. "You're okay." Then she looked at his chest. "Are you okay?"

He looked down at his chest, which was very bloody now. "Not really, no, but I'm alive."

She wrung out her hands, clenching them into fists and releasing them as she headed in the kitchen. " There were rags in here. Towels. To stop the blood."

"Let's just go," said Reilly. "We have to get out of here."

She snatched up a rag and went to him, pushing the fabric into his wounds.

It hurt. He gasped.

"Sorry," she said. "But you apply pressure. That's what you do. We need to find something to tie them down and to bandage you."

"We need to *go*," he said.

Her fingers fluttered around his face. " I thought you were dead. I thought they killed you. They said something about giving Hawk your skin."

Reilly grimaced. " And here I thought Hawk and I bonded."

Wren laughed. She laughed high and wild and then she stopped. "Are they dead?" She started ripping at one of the rags, turning it into strips of fabric. "Did you kill them?"

" I don't know. Not the woman," said Reilly. "But I stabbed the man a couple times. He went down. I think it's really hard to stab someone to death, though."

Wren stretched one of the fabric strips around Reilly's chest, trying to tie to it off. "Hell, why do you have to have such a broad chest, Reilly?"

"Just leave it." He pushed her away and headed for the

door. "Let's go."

* * *

"Which way?" said Wren. They were in the woods, back on the other side of the clearing where the pavilion was. They knew they'd come this way.

"Um..." Reilly looked one way and then the other. "I can't remember. I feel too woozy. It's probably blood loss." He glanced at her. "What's your excuse?"

"I don't know. I'm shit with directions?"

"Well, that's great."

"I guess you don't have your phone anymore?"

"No, the asshole who was trying to skin me alive took it," said Reilly.

"Well, maybe it's still on him," said Wren. "Maybe we should go back to the pavilion, and look."

"No," said Reilly. "I saw that movie, and what happened was, when they got back to the spot, the killer was gone, and they both got axed to death. Or chainsawed."

"Yeah? Well, I saw the movie where the people wandered aimlessly in the woods for days until the killer cornered them in a weird old house and killed them all."

Reilly looked back in the direction of the pavilion.

Wren did too. Then she turned back to the woods. She pointed. "I think it's this way."

"When we were back in the cabin, we should have gone out and seen if Miller was alive," said Reilly. "Maybe he had his phone on him. Or his gun."

"I guess they took your gun too?"

"Sure as hell did."

Wren started walking in the direction she'd pointed. Reilly came with her. "This seems like the right way. We're going to be fine."

"Yeah, we'll get out of the woods, and we'll call this in," said Wren. "There are two innocent little girls out here at the mercy of Hawk, and we need to do something to save them."

"What?" said Reilly. "Girls?" Then he nodded. "The beds. They have daughters?"

"Yeah," said Wren. "They're eleven. They're twins. They're Hawk's wet dream."

"Oh, gross," said Reilly.

"We need to stop it," said Wren.

"Not to mention the fact that we can't be sure that Anderson is dead, or that Miller is. And Roger is roaming around in the woods somewhere."

"Maybe he got out," said Wren.

"Maybe he did," said Reilly. "What are the odds he went to the police?"

"Um, I put it twenty to one against," said Wren. "I don't think he much likes the police."

"Hell," said Reilly.

They trudged through the woods in silence for a while.

"Hey." Wren pointed. "The path. That's the path. Right there. Up ahead."

"Oh, hell, you're right," said Reilly. "We made it."

It was only a few feet until they made it back onto the narrow path, the one that Hawk and Major had cleared out to get to Hawk's house. Now on the path, Wren felt sure that she knew the way. To the right led further into the woods. To the left was back to civilization. She turned left and started walking, Reilly right behind her.

Up ahead, the path went around a tall rock formation, and when they rounded the bend, a body was swinging from the branches of one of the trees.

It was Roger.

His throat had been cut and he wasn't wearing a shirt. There was a pattern carved into his skin, shaky lines connected to each other, like forks of lightning or antlers. Where his eyes should have been, there was nothing but red holes.

CHAPTER TWENTY-FIVE

They stopped short.

Wren gaped at it, horrified and fascinated, as usual.

Reilly moaned.

Wren turned her head to one side, staring at the pattern on the chest. It was like the drawings he'd made in his apartment, the ones on the walls.

Reilly shoved her. "Go," he said in a guttural voice.

"We can't leave him like this," said Wren. "Where's the knife? Cut him down."

"It's a crime scene, Wren," said Reilly. "Remember what you said to Miller?"

"Oh, yeah," said Wren, who couldn't seem to tear her gaze away from Roger's body.

"Go," he said. "We need to get free and get to a phone. We'll have this woods swarming with police in an hour."

"No, you won't," said a voice from behind them.

They whirled.

Karen was on the path, holding Reilly's gun, pointing it at both of them. Behind her was Terrence, barely on his feet, his clothes stained in blood. He had Miller's gun and had it trained on them as well. His hand was trembling.

"Yeah," said Reilly. "I knew it was hard as hell to stab a man to death."

Karen's nose was red. "I felt sorry for you, black man. But you tried to kill my husband."

"Well, he tried to kill me first, to be fair," said Reilly.

Wren furrowed her brow. "When did you have time to

catch Roger and kill him?" She gestured with her thumb at the body handing behind him.

"Hawk did that," said Karen.

Terrence coughed. Blood came up. He spat it on the path.

"We have to kill the black one and give Wren to Hawk," said Karen. "It's for our little girls. We don't have a choice."

"You do have a choice," said Wren. "It's like I was saying before. You wanted to believe me, Karen. You've never wanted this. It's Terrence—"

"He didn't want it either," yelled Karen. "He hates it as much as I do."

"Does he?" said Wren. "Of the two of you, who's idea was it to go to the police?"

Karen licked her lips. "Well... it was both of us."

"Really?" said Wren. "Was it little Felix Wilson? That night at the Walker's? You saw him shot in the head, still clutching his toys, and you knew what you were doing, it couldn't be in the service of anything good. You knew that it had to end. Vivian had to be stopped."

Karen swallowed. "Terrence agreed with me. He wanted Vivian gone."

"Oh, I see," said Wren, looking over Karen's shoulder at Terrence. "You thought you could take over for her. But then you started realizing, now that the police were involved, that the whole FCL was going to crumble, and you wouldn't have anything. So, you cut your losses. Sure, it would have been nice to have a whole cult to order around, but you'd settle for your wife and kids, huh? And the killing? Well, you just like the killing, don't you?"

Terrence laughed. His teeth were red. "You think you understand me, but you don't. It's not me that needs the killing, little Wren. It's the Lord. He's the one who guides our path. Shoot them, Karen. We'll shoot Hawk too. We have guns now."

Karen turned to look at Terrence. "But Hawk... you said he was in the service of the Lord."

"Not if he takes our girls," said Terrence. "Not then."

"Don't shoot us," said Wren. "Please, don't shoot us. Let us go and get help."

"No one's getting help," said Karen.

"Shoot them," said Terrence.

Karen turned on him. She marched over to her husband and snatched his gun out of his hand. "No one's getting shot either." She looked at Wren and Reilly. "Not as long as you do as I say. I'm taking you both to Hawk. If he wants the black man dead so bad, he can do it himself." She gestured with her gun. "Let's go. Walk."

"I don't think you'll shoot me," said Wren.

"No?" said Karen, and pulled the trigger.

CHAPTER TWENTY-SIX

The gun went off with a crack, and the bullet lodged in the trunk of a tree too close to Wren for comfort. It splintered the tree, sending shards of wood everywhere.

Wren cowered.

Reilly staggered.

Terrence fell backwards and settled on the ground. He began to cough again.

"You okay?" said Karen to him.

"Save our girls," he croaked. "Save our babies, darling."

Karen nodded. She gestured with the gun. "Let's go."

Wren started to move.

Reilly did too, but he stumbled.

Wren reached out to catch him.

Karen yelled.

"I'm just helping him," said Wren. "Just let him lean on me."

"Fine," Karen snapped. "Walk."

So, they walked.

They left Terrence behind. He sat on the path, his back against a tree trunk, and his breath came in rattling gasps.

Reilly leaned against Wren, and he was bleeding through the makeshift bandages she'd put on him, not that they were put on very well. They probably would have fallen off, but they were stuck to his skin with his own crusted blood.

Karen came behind them, gun on them, telling them to move faster if they faltered. Other than that, no one spoke.

They walked and walked, and the path went on and on. Wren couldn't keep track of how long it was. Reilly was heavy against her, and he was sweaty and panting. She was worried. She thought he'd lost too much blood. She clutched at him, wondering how it had all gone so badly, so fast. Her breath grew labored too, and sweat broke out on her forehead and at the nape of her neck.

They walked.

Eventually, a house came into view. Well, it was charitable to call it a house. It was more like a pyramid with doors and a few holes for windows. It was covered in black pitch. Maybe he'd done that to waterproof it.

When the house came into view, Karen yelled for Hawk.

And Hawk appeared in the doorway to the house. He looked more gaunt than Wren remembered. Had he always been that thin and skeletal? He looked her over, his gray eyes piercing her, but his face expressionless.

"Where are my girls?" Karen's voice was thin.

"They're sleeping," said Hawk, coming out of the pyramid and walking toward them. "Where's your husband?"

"Dead, most likely," said Karen. "I'll shoot you too, Hawk. You deserve it."

Hawk advanced on them, his gray eyes flashing. "You'll do no such thing, Karen Marie Freeman. Hand me that gun."

"No," said Karen, shaking her head, backing away.

"I command thee, sister," said Hawk. "Turn it over to me, the agent of thy lord and master, for I am most displeased. I will spare thy life if thou dost obey."

Karen crumpled to the ground, sobbing, holding the gun above her head.

Hawk pushed past Wren and took the gun from her. "Fucking idiots just roll over if you start talking like the King James version. Really, Karen?"

She whimpered.

Hawk shot her in the head.

Karen fell backwards, eyes staring blankly at the sky.

Wren jumped.

Hawk whirled around, leveling the gun at Reilly. "Wren, you're in my way. This one is supposed to be dead."

Reilly glared at Hawk. "It's because I wouldn't give you a job, isn't it? Listen, Hawk, you have no experience. Why would I let you work in law enforcement, huh? What are your qualifications? Just that you're really good at making people shoot themselves?"

Hawk stalked forward, putting the barrel of the gun between Reilly's eyes. "Shut up."

"Hawk," said Wren.

He turned to her.

"What are you doing?" she said.

He raised his eyebrows. " Killing the witnesses, little bird."

She sucked in a breath. "Don't. We should talk. We've never talked, not honestly, not when I knew everything."

He lifted his chin, surveying her. "Talk, hmm? Honestly, hmm? I don't think you can *be* honest, little bird. I think your whole identity is caught up in lying to yourself."

She forced herself to smile. "You want someone to know how you did it, don't you? You want to tell me about that."

Hawk chuckled. "Oh, little bird. You think it's like that, don't you? I'm not like your other killers. And it's not that I want to tell, it's that you want to know. Ever since you saw that dead little girl in the Walker house, you 've been salivating for all the details. It gets you wet."

She flinched.

"Now, what's going to happen is that I'm going to shoot the detective here, and then you can spend as much time with the dead body as you want. Because we both know you want to."

She swallowed. "Not Reilly. Please? Not him?"

" Has to be him," said Hawk. He shifted on his feet, looking down at Reilly. "Got to say, before all this, I was a little squeamish about it. I liked it to be clean. But I find you get desensitized to it. The more you kill, the easier it gets."

"Not Reilly," she said.

"Why not Reilly?" Hawk was glaring at the man.

"Maybe she likes me better than you," Reilly said.

"Shut up," said Wren, panicked. "Don't talk, Reilly."

"Is that it, little bird? Do you like him better?" Hawk turned to look at her. "You want him?"

"No," said Wren. "No, no. It's not like that at all. It's you, Hawk. It's always been you. It's only ever been you. Hawk, please. Don't shoot him. Just talk to me. We have things to talk about."

"We can't talk until he's dead."

"Hawk, please. I don't want to be surrounded by any more death. I'm... I'm pregnant."

Hawk's eyes widened. He hadn't been expecting that. "What?"

"I forgot my birth control," she said. "I didn't mean to, and then I forgot the condoms, and then... I'm just a mess. And I need you right now, Hawk, I need you not to be killing people. Okay?"

Hawk pulled the gun away from Reilly's head and put the safety on. He tucked it into his belt. "That's a whole lot of stupid, little bird."

Her mouth was dry. "I-I know."

Hawk advanced on her. "Not just your stupid, of course. Not fair to let you bear the burden alone. It takes two." And then he balled up his fist and punched her in the stomach. Hard.

CHAPTER TWENTY-SEVEN

Wren gasped.
Hawk held onto her shoulder and punched her again.
She cried out.
His lips at her ear. "If it doesn't take," he whispered, "get rid of it as soon as you can." He let go of her.
She doubled over, clutching her stomach, grunting.
Reilly lurched at Hawk. "You fucking bastard—"
Hawk punched Reilly too.
Reilly staggered backward.
Hawk kicked him, knocking Reilly onto his back. He kicked Reilly again, boot to the face.
Reilly's nose erupted red gore.
"No!" said Wren.
Reilly twitched and then was still. His wide eyes gazed at the sky.
Hawk looked at her.
She shook her head at him. "No," she repeated, softer.
Hawk turned his back on her and started walking toward the doorway of the house.
Wren straightened painfully. It hurt where Hawk had hit her. And there was something wet and warm running down her thigh. *My period,* she thought. *Must be that.* She didn't have anything out here to deal with it.
But her dignity didn't seem important at the moment, not with Reilly lying motionless on the ground, and the dead body of Karen behind her, and the little girls that Hawk had said were sleeping.

Funny, though. Funny your period started right then.

Wren shook her head, dislodging the thought. She didn't have time to think about any of that. She went to Reilly, kneeling next to him, seizing his wrist, feeling for a pulse.

A faint sound from the house—a girl's voice, frightened.

Wren dropped Reilly's hand and rushed for the doorway. "Hawk, don't you dare hurt those girls, don't you *dare*."

Inside the house, it was dark. The only light came from tiny windows. She couldn't see at first, but then she made out one small figure lying on the floor, and then she saw another, this one moving, trying to get up.

Hawk's voice from the darkness. "It's all ruined now."

Wren went to the little girl. She held out her hand.

The little girl grasped it.

Wren tried to pull the girl to her feet, but the girl wasn't trying hard enough. She was too sluggish. Wren got down to her knees, trying to get the girl's arm around her shoulder, wondering how she was going to get the girl's sister.

Hawk crouched down in front of her, his features shadowed. "At first, I thought I could get you back to stop it. I thought you'd make it better. And you did, you *did*."

"Out of the way, Hawk." She was still struggling with the little girl, who wasn't speaking, but was now making high-pitched mewling noises. Oh, hell, did the sedative Hawk gave them do brain damage? Why didn't she know this?

"But then you came to me that night and you told me that you killed a man and you *liked* it."

She flinched.

He leaned closer, and now a sliver of sunlight from the window illuminated half his face. "And then I knew that you weren't saving me, that I—that *he*—was getting to you. Getting into your head." He reached out and touched her temple. "Inside here."

"Get your hands off me," she said through clenched teeth.

171

He pulled his fingers away. "I grappled with it. I wasn't sure which way to go. I had tried to resist, but if he had you too, maybe it wouldn't be so bad. I thought, maybe we could be there together."

"Be where?" she said, even though she shouldn't engage him, even though it was idiotic to talk to him right now, when he wasn't making any sense.

"Wherever the Horned Lord is," said Hawk.

"No," she said, her face twisting in disgust. "No, you don't get to play that stupid card. You don't get to blame this on some imaginary man with horns. He's not real, and he didn't do this. You did. It was you. You killed people, Hawk. You killed *little girls*. You were killing me over and over again. Killing me because you wanted to fuck me. Well, you got your shot, didn't you? Got me to spread my legs, and you thought it would stop the compulsion, but you had to face the fact that you just like killing, you sick fuck—"

"That's wrong." He shook his head. "You don't understand anything."

"I don't need to understand. Now, get out of my way, because I'm not letting you hurt these girls."

"You've never seen his face," said Hawk. "You've never been alone when his shadow falls over you. You don't know what it's like, the way he makes your insides twist, how you can hardly breathe in his presence—"

"The Crimson Ram is *imaginary*." She was screaming it. "Some stupid made-up god, the shared vision of David Song and Vivian. They made him up so that they could control people."

"I *wish* he was imaginary." Now Hawk was yelling too, and there was a desperate edge to his voice. "You don't understand, Wren, she protected you."

"Oh, bullshit, stop—"

"Your mother, she kept you away from him. She never let you see him—"

"Did you see him while you were tripping on acid?" said

Wren.

"It doesn't matter whether you saw him or not," said Hawk. "He's in you. Working through you. Making you do his bidding. He wants sacrifices, and you like to kill, so you'll kill again. You'll kill for him, and you'll never even know you're doing it—"

"No." She hated him. She hated him because he was saying her worst fears out loud, and she worried that if they were given words, given form, there would be more power to them, and they would overtake her.

"I didn't *want* to kill those girls." He was anguished. " But the Crimson Ram was angry, because you were protected. He wanted you. I was there when Vivian was told what he wanted of you, and she changed it all. She defied the Horned Lord and had you given to me, in the pairing, and I was supposed to protect you, and I did. I did what I could, but..." He shook his head. "The Lord wasn't done with me. He made me take those other girls."

"What you're calling the Crimson Ram is just a part of yourself," she said.

"Then it's a part of you, too," he said. "That part of you that felt triumph when you pulled the trigger?"

"It might be part of me, but it came from *her*," said Wren.

"Vivian?"

"Yes."

And then they were quiet.

"It's ruined now," he finally said. "I thought we could be together, could... could kill together. That maybe it would be okay if it was both of us. I tried to kill the sort of people you would want dead."

" You mean Oliver? And Noah Adams? Did you kill him?"

"Noah killed himself," said Hawk darkly.

"But you were there."

"I was," he said. "For you."

"No, no, no." She shook her head fiercely. "You don't get

to pin this on me. It's not about me. You did this, all on your own. And I would never have killed with you. That's disgusting."

"No," he said. "Not after what I did to your unborn child. Not anymore."

"Not ever," she said.

His hand shot out and he seized her by the neck.

She choked.

He flung her against the wall of the house, and she collided there, gasping for breath, hurt.

He pushed the little girl back onto the floor of the house and he wrapped his hand around her neck.

"No!" screamed Wren, getting up and launching herself at him.

She tackled him and they went backwards on the floor. She was on top of him, her body pressed against his, and it was familiar and horrible and terrifying and it caught her off guard.

And he flipped them, so that now he was on top of her, his pelvis crushing hers, his gray eyes wild as he looked down on her.

She struggled. She raked her nails over his cheek.

He wrapped his hands around her neck, tight.

She couldn't breathe. The world was going dark, now, everything was closing in on her. The periphery of her vision faded and faded...

She scrabbled at his face. She got her thumb into his mouth, scraping at the inside of his gums.

He grunted, and jerked his head back. At the same time, his grip on her neck loosened, he moved his body back from hers.

She brought up her knee into his crotch.

He yelled.

She punched him.

And now they had switched again. She had rolled on top of him, and he was under her, and he was in pain. She hit him again. And again. She couldn't stop hitting him.

"Little bird," he moaned.

She slammed her fist into his nose. "Don't call me that."

"Wren," he breathed.

She pushed up from his body and got to her feet. She kicked him. In the stomach. In the chest. Under his chin.

Then she spied the gun he'd taken from Karen, peering out of the top of his belt, and she felt stupid for not remembering it sooner. She snatched it up and turned it on him.

He gazed up at her. His nose was bleeding. He chuckled. "Going to shoot me?"

She cocked the gun.

"You probably should," he said, and his voice dropped in register several notches. "You probably want to."

"Maybe I do," she breathed.

"You think I want to kill *you*, don't you?" he whispered. "You think that's what this is all about. But maybe it's about you, little bird. Maybe it's about coming full circle and taking your place at his right hand. Maybe the reason he wanted me to kill was just for this moment, for you to kill me and complete the arc."

She didn't say anything. Her blood was thundering against her temples, pulsing in time to a remembered drum beat.

"Do it, Wren," he rasped. "Pull the trigger. Take my life."

But instead, she uncocked the gun and turned in her hand and brought down the butt of it against the top of his head as hard as she could.

He let out a little sound of surprise, reaching for her.

She clocked him again, even harder this time.

And he slithered onto the ground, unconscious.

CHAPTER TWENTY-EIGHT

Wren panted.

She sat down on the ground, putting her head between her knees, and she tried to get her breathing under control. That was all she could concentrate on for the moment.

Then she lifted her head to look at the twin girls.

One of the girls was sitting up, looking right at Wren. The other was twitching.

Wren motioned to the girl sitting up. "Can you stand? Stand up."

The girl looked down at Hawk's motionless form, and then she scrambled to her feet. She ran over to her sister and took the other girl by the shoulders, shaking her. "Wake up, Nattie. Wake up."

The other girl moaned.

Wren got up and went over to the girls. "Are you okay?"

"The milkshake tastes funny," moaned the girl on the ground.

"Wake up, Nattie." Panic in the other girl's voice. She glanced at Wren with panicked eyes. She shot a look down at the gun and then up at Wren's eyes.

Wren tucked the gun away. She held out her hand. "I'm not going to hurt you. But we have to get you out of here."

Nattie sat up, sputtering. She blinked.

The other girl pulled Nattie to her feet. " We have to run." And she darted out of the house, dragging her sister along behind her.

"Wait!" Wren called. "You don't want to go out there.

Your mother—"

A scream.

Wren tore out of the house to find the girls staring down at their mother's body. They were both horrified.

Reilly! She had never gotten his pulse.

She turned to look for his body.

But Reilly was gone.

CHAPTER TWENTY-NINE

Wren didn't know what that meant. Had Reilly gotten up and left? Would he have done that? Why wouldn't he have come into the house and tried to help her with Hawk?

What about Terrence? Maybe he'd somehow recovered enough to come and drag Reilly's body away. Maybe he was skinning him or carving him up. She needed to go and find Reilly now, save him. She couldn't let anything happen to Reilly.

The girls looked back at the house and then at the body of their mother, and they didn't know what to do.

Wren couldn't think about Reilly right now. She had to take care of these innocent children. They were caught in the middle of all of this through no fault of their own. Reilly was a cop. He'd signed up for this, and as much as she wanted to find him, her priority had to be the girls.

Wren went to them, kneeling down. "Hi," she said.

The girls both shied away from her. They had tears glittering in their eyes. Lord, they must be so frightened.

"I'm Wren." She touched her chest. "What are your names?"

The girls exchanged a glance, and unspoken communication seemed to pass between them. They were likely trying to decide if they could trust Wren. They didn't know her, after all, and they were in a living nightmare. But they seemed to decide to take what they could get.

"Jessica," said one of the girls. "And this is Natalie."

"Okay, Jessica and Natalie," said Wren. "We need to get

out of here. Get somewhere safe, away from the man back there." She pointed at the house. "Will you come with me?"

"Daddy?" said Natalie. "Where's Daddy?"

Even if Terrence was still alive, no way was Wren giving the girls back to that man. He was insane. But there was no reason to further traumatize them. "We'll find your father later, okay? Will you come with me now?"

The girls hesitated, but then they nodded.

Wren held out her hand.

Jessica took it, and Natalie gripped Jessica's hand.

Wren led them in a wide berth around their mother's body and back onto the path. As they walked, she considered the idea that Terrence was still sitting on the path, where they'd left him, and she didn't want the girls to have to see that too. But she didn't know what else she could do. They had to stay on the path if they wanted to get out of the woods. She considered telling the girls to stay put when they got close, and then going up ahead on her own.

But she didn't want to leave them alone. They might run off, and she didn't know how long Hawk would be out. She'd hit him hard, but she knew he wasn't dead. He'd wake up, and he'd come after them.

Or he'd flee.

He'd get away.

That made her angry, too. He shouldn't be allowed to get away. She considered leaving the girls where they were, going back to the house and putting a bullet in Hawk Marner.

That was probably the smart thing to do.

But she wasn't going to do that, and she was going to tell herself that she wasn't doing it because she didn't want to be a killer, and not because her feelings about Hawk were confusing and twisted.

She didn't want to think about that.

She should probably talk to the girls. She tried to think of something reassuring to say, but she didn't know what could possibly comfort them in the wake of their mother's death and their own near brush with death themselves.

When Vivian had been arrested, she'd still been left with her dad, and he was the parent who had shown her affection and love. Wren suspected the dynamic was switched here, so they were truly alone in the world, and they must be feeling such terror and such sadness. What could she possibly say that would reassure them?

No, there was nothing.

She only hoped the girls would continue to walk with her. She was going to take them out of the woods, and she didn't think the girls had even been out of the woods. They'd been here their entire lives.

A noise, in the distance.

Someone was coming down the path. Wren could hear their footsteps, hear them moving through the underbrush.

CHAPTER THIRTY

Wren tugged on Jessica's hand, pulling the girls off the path.

They came with her, and they crouched down behind a thorn bush. It was probably Terrence, and if it was, the girls were going to run to him, and Wren didn't know what she would do. She had a gun. She could shoot Terrence if necessary, but she wasn't going to shoot the girls' father in front of them if she could help it.

But if it meant saving Reilly, if her own life was in danger—

A uniformed police officer appeared around the bend. He wasn't alone. At least ten other men and women were following him, all in full uniform and with bullet-proof vests from the look of their bulky chests.

Reilly was with them.

He was bringing up the rear, and his face was smeared with blood. He had a shirt on now, but she could see the makeshift bandages she'd tied to him peering out of the collar. He looked awful, but he was upright, and he was moving.

She stood up, waving at him. "Reilly!"

"Wren!" he said,

Wren pulled the girls out from behind the thorn bush, practically running for Reilly. " You were gone, and I thought you were… I thought he came and dragged you off."

Reilly hurried over to her. "I'm sorry I didn't go in after

you. I came to, and I looked into the house, and you were talking at him, and I thought I should go back for the phones, call in help. It was a gamble, but I was unarmed and wounded, and I didn't know if I would have been any help if I did go in—"

"You did the right thing," said Wren.

Two officers had peeled away from the rest and they were coming over to Wren and Reilly.

"Detective Reilly, since we've found them, let's get you all back out of the woods," said one. The officer turned to Wren. "We tried to convince him to go out and get medical attention, but he was dead set on making sure you were all right."

Wren hugged him.

He hugged her back. Then he grunted. He was wounded, after all.

She pulled back. "You did exactly the right thing."

He gave her a weary smile. "I took a gamble. But I had a pretty good idea you could hold your own. You got away."

"Let's get out of these damned woods," she said.

* * *

"You sure you want to do this, Mr. Reilly?" said the nurse, who was holding out a clipboard to him.

"The doctor said that I could, didn't he?" said Reilly.

"Yes, but he recommended a night for observation, just to be sure."

"I've got some stitches and a bandaged nose."

"Some of your wounds are deep," said the nurse. "You lost a lot of blood."

"I'll be more comfortable at home," said Reilly.

"As long as you have someone there who can keep an eye on you and call for help if something happens."

"Sure," said Reilly. "Of course." He gestured to the clipboard. "Where do I sign?"

The nurse pointed out the places for signatures and initialing, and then he was free. He'd signed himself out of the hospital. Wearing his sweaty, bloody pants and a sweatshirt from the hospital gift shop, he staggered out into the afternoon light.

He'd decided to check himself out after Lopez had come by to fill him in on everything that had been happening. He asked Lopez to go and talk to Wren, too. She deserved to be kept up to speed. But Lopez said that Wren had been discharged from the hospital.

Wren didn't have a phone anymore. It had been taken by the Freemans. He'd gotten his phone back when he left to call for help, but he couldn't even call her.

So, there was nothing to do but go and find her.

He could have sent someone else to talk to Wren, he supposed, but he felt like he should be the one to do it.

He had an Uber pick him up from the hospital and take him to Wren's place.

She opened the door when he knocked. "Reilly, geez, why aren't you in the hospital?"

"I'm fine," he said. "I signed myself out."

"You were stabbed *a lot* and your nose... is your nose broken?"

He gingerly fingered the bandage. "They set it. It's fine. Anyway, what about *your* nose?"

"Not broken. Bled a lot, hurt like a bitch, but fine now." She opened the door wider. "Well, come in. You're crazy, and you should go back to the hospital, but if you're insisting on being stupid, you better come in."

He did.

She shut the door behind them, gesturing to her couch. "Sit."

He sat.

She came and sat down opposite him on an easy chair. "Did they tell you anything?"

"What do you want to know?"

"When they got to the house, was he there?"

"Hawk?" said Reilly. "Yes, he was. He was out of it,

barely coming to, and they didn't have any trouble subduing him. He's in custody for shooting Karen in the head. The rest of it, we don't know if we have a case yet."

"You mean, he's not being charged with the other murders?"

"Not yet."

"Does that mean you didn't find any evidence out there? No trophies, nothing like that?"

"Nothing," said Reilly. "We need to get back to the office, regroup, see what we can put together. But it might not matter. We both watched him shoot that woman in the head. That's murder, and it's ironclad. Maybe it's enough."

"But Major," she said. "If he's innocent…"

"Yeah," said Reilly. "Well, we'll work on it."

"Was he…?" She shook her head.

Reilly waited.

She never finished the sentence.

"How are you?" he said. "This has to be a lot for you."

"I'm not great," she said wryly.

"Yeah," he murmured.

They were quiet for several long moments.

"The girls? Jessica and Natalie?"

"They're with Child Protective Services," said Reilly. "I don't know more than that, unfortunately."

"Terrence? What about him? Did they find him?"

"He's dead," said Reilly. "He bled out in the woods."

"So, the girls are orphans."

"Yeah, they are."

"Those poor girls. They're all alone."

"They're free from their crazy parents who were probably feeding them human flesh," said Reilly.

"That's true," said Wren. "But it's all they've ever known. Do you think they'd let me see them?"

"I can't see why not."

"I don't know if I'd be any help or not," said Wren, "but I feel like… I can't stop thinking about them. I'm worried about them."

"You should go and see them, then," said Reilly. "You should definitely do that."

"I think I will." She gave him a wan smile. And then it faded. "The other officers. Anderson? Miller? Did either of them make it?"

Reilly shook his head. "Unfortunately, no."

"Hell," said Wren.

"There are going to be memorial services," said Reilly. "We'll go."

"Of course," said Wren. "We owe them that. They were working for the task force when this happened. We put them in danger."

"We did." Reilly studied his knuckles.

"In some ways, their deaths are on us," she said softly. "In some ways, it's like we killed them."

"We didn't," said Reilly. He raised his gaze to hers. "But I did kill Terrence. I stabbed him, and he bled out, and if it weren't for that, he'd be alive. I killed a man."

Her lips parted and she gazed at him.

Reilly couldn't keep eye contact. He looked back at his knuckles. "I had to. He was trying to kill me."

"You did. You absolutely had to. You shouldn't feel..."

"Guilty?" said Reilly, looking back up at her.

"No," she said.

"Did you feel guilty after you shot Kyler Morris?"

Now she was the one who wouldn't look at him. "Why are you asking me that?"

"I, uh, I don't," said Reilly. "Feel guilty."

She looked up. "No?"

"No," said Reilly. "He... when I was doing it, it wasn't like he was a human being, it was like ... like he was a monster. Or an animal. We were both animals. I was the prey, and he was hunting me, and it was..." He raised his shoulders and dropped them. "What I feel, mostly, is terrified. Still. Afraid that he's out there in the shadows somewhere, waiting for me. Afraid that I didn't kill him after all. It's kind of…" He sucked in a breath. "I've never felt afraid like this."

She got up from her chair and went and sat next to him on the couch. They didn't touch.

He looked away. "Listen to me, going on about this when you're dealing with all of the fallout from Hawk. I shouldn't—"

"You've been through hell, too, Reilly." She put her hand on his shoulder.

He turned to face her. "Yeah, but how are you?"

She laughed a little. "Peachy."

He leaned his head back on her couch.

They were quiet.

"I can't believe you signed yourself out of the hospital."

"They told me it was fine as long as I had someone to watch me," he said.

"But you don't!" She sat up straight, turning sideways on the couch to face him. "You have to stay here. I'll take the couch, and you can sleep in my bed. Unless that's weird. I mean, if you'd rather the couch—" She broke off. "I guess you'd actually go to Maliah's, right?"

"Uh…" He dragged a hand over the top of his head. He didn't know what the hell was going on with him and Maliah, and he was pretty sure a night on Wren Delacroix's couch wasn't going to earn him any points with his girlfriend. Was Maliah his girlfriend?

"I can drive you to her place," said Wren. "You didn't come in your car, and you shouldn't be driving anyway."

He patted the couch. "This thing seems pretty comfy."

Wren gave him a crooked smile. "Yeah? You want to stay?"

"Sure."

"Good," she said. "I'd rather not be alone. Also, if Terrence Freeman is a zombie and comes to the door, scratching to get in, I can protect you."

"Really?" He shook his head at her. "I confide in you, and you mock me?"

She winked at him. "It's our dynamic, Reilly. I can't help it."

"I see how it is." He picked up one of the cushions on the couch and hurled it at her.

She ducked, squealing.

* * *

Wren opened the door to headquarters for Reilly.

He walked in, glowering at her. "You know, I'm not an invalid."

"No, but how many times were you stabbed again? Like five times?"

He stalked down the hallway. "You could have taken me to my car. I could have driven."

"Relax, I'll drive you to your place after work," said Wren. "It's really not that big of a deal."

He turned and pointed at her. "If I can't drive, then I'm probably not in any shape to be at work, am I?"

Wren spread her hands. "It was your idea to come in. You said, 'Let's get coffee,' and then while we were at the coffee shop, you said we might as well check in at headquarters, and so here we are." She lifted her caramel double-shot latte to her lips and took a sip.

"Yeah, well, I want my car."

"Is it because you feel emasculated without it?" said Wren. "Without the car, you're missing something, like, I don't know, your penis?"

Reilly guffawed, spewing coffee all over his shirt, which was still the hoodie he'd purchased at the hospital gift shop. He wiped at the back of his mouth. "Okay, that was uncalled for. When have I ever—"

The door to Maliah's office opened.

Wren saw Reilly's eyes widen and he stopped speaking.

"Oh, don't let me interrupt your banter," said Maliah dryly. "What were you talking about? Cai's dick?"

Wren glanced back and forth between the two of them. "Okay, well, I think I'll just be going down to my office now." She gestured, plastering a big smile on her face.

"Wait, Delacroix," said Maliah, and she suddenly sounded chagrined.

Wren raised her eyebrows at the other woman.

"I heard about Hawk. About… everything," said Maliah. "I'm really sorry. I can't imagine how you must be feeling right now."

Wren felt a lump rising in her throat. Her face twisted. She looked down at her coffee cup.

Now the silence was deafening.

Wren struggled to get herself under control. "I, uh, I really do have… things… in my office." She turned and fled.

* * *

Reilly gazed at Maliah.

She sighed, staring after Wren. "Shit, that was the wrong thing to say, too." She eyed Reilly. "I suppose you know *just* how to comfort her."

"Hey, Maliah, this isn't what it looks like," said Reilly.

"You haven't been home," said Maliah. "You don't have your car. You're wearing…" She looked him over. "What *are* you wearing?"

"Wren took my pants while I was sleeping and washed them," said Reilly. "So, they're clean."

Maliah raised her eyebrows.

"I mean, she didn't take them off me," said Reilly. "They were already off."

Maliah raised her eyebrows higher.

"I took them off and folded them. And set them next to the couch. Where I slept."

Maliah crossed her arms over her chest.

"Look, nothing happened. I went there because I needed to fill her in. And then, it was late, and they told me at the hospital it would be better if I wasn't alone, in case something happened."

"Yeah, I went looking for you at the hospital," said Maliah. "You didn't even call me to tell me that you left."

Reilly rubbed his forehead.

"I don't think this is going to work, Cai," Maliah said softly.

His gaze snapped up to meet hers. "Look, Maliah, it isn't like you're thinking."

"I know," she said. "Delacroix's a piece of work, but she's not ready to hop under the sheets with you, not after everything she's been through. I can tell that."

"Okay, good," he said. "There's nothing between her and me."

"It's platonic, right?"

"Right."

She nodded. "I believe you."

"Okay, then... So?"

"We don't work," she said.

"We haven't even really tried," he said. "And besides there are..." He lowered his voice. "*Things* that work very well between us."

She smiled a little, but it was a sad smile. "You're right. We have that, Cai, and it's good, but it's all we have. We have nothing in common. We have nothing to talk about. We're not in love with each other. We were running *away* from things, and we ran into each other's arms. We were never running *towards* each other."

He opened his mouth to disagree, but he didn't say anything, because she was right. They really didn't have anything in common besides work.

"We work together," she said. "I don't want it to be awkward with us. I feel like... if we kept trying at this, we'd get more entangled, and it would be even more painful when everything broke up. Better to end it now. Better to move on."

His jaw worked. "Maybe you're right," he told the carpet.

CHAPTER THIRTY-ONE

Someone was rapping on the door to Wren's office. She swiped at her eyes, rubbing the heels of her hands over her tears. Taking a deep breath, she got up and opened the door.

It was Reilly. He saw her, and creased his brow. "Hey, are you—"

"Fine," she said brusquely. "I'm fine. What about you? You in deep shit? You want me to talk to Maliah, explain that—"

"She just dumped me," said Reilly.

"Oh, hell!" Wren put her hands on her hips. "That's not even cool. I am going to talk to her and tell her that I have no interest in—"

"It's probably a good thing," said Reilly. "I think I was only pursuing that relationship to make myself feel better."

"What?"

"You know, if it was real between Maliah and me, like if we were in love, then it was less horrible what I did to Janessa."

"Oh," said Wren.

"But it wasn't real," said Reilly. "It never was."

"I'm sorry," said Wren.

"No, it's cool," said Reilly. "I'm fine. I came down here, because I assume we have work to do."

"Right," she said. "Evidence. We need evidence from Hawk. Or a confession? Maybe a confession? I mean, he confessed to me in the house out there, and I saw him trying to hurt those girls. But something formal and signed, that would be better."

"Are you ready to go and see him? To talk to him?"

She hesitated.

"Let's table that idea for now," said Reilly. "Like I said, we've got him for Karen Freeman's murder. He's not going anywhere. We have time to build a case against him."

"But what about Major?" said Wren. "If he's innocent, we need to get him out. And he might be able to help us build the case against Hawk. I think I could handle going and talking to him right now."

"Okay," said Reilly. "But if we do that, you're taking me back to my place first. I definitely need a change of clothes."

* * *

The superintendent of the Eastern Regional Jail and Correctional Facility cleared his throat. "Listen, this is all highly irregular."

Reilly straightened his tie. "You bet it is. We've been here lots of times to talk to inmates in custody, and we've never had to go through the warden."

"Superintendent," said the superintendent. "That's my title. I thought it best that I talk directly to you about this. You see, we can't honor your request to talk to Major Hill, because Mr. Hill is, unfortunately, deceased."

Wren's lips parted. What?

Reilly glanced at her and then back at the superintendent. "What are you talking about? We were here with him days ago. He was fine then. What happened? How can he be dead?"

"Hung himself," said the superintendent. "He used sheets from his bed. It happened last night."

Wren's voice came out scratchy. "Did he have any contact with Hawk Marner?"

"Marner?" said the superintendent. "He was just brought in. Hill, on the other hand, has been here for quite some time. I can't see any reason why they would have interacted with each other. It would go against proper procedure."

"Hawk found a way," Reilly said flatly.

"Hawk talked Major into it," said Wren. "He can do that, you said. You saw him do that."

"But why?" said Reilly. Now, they were talking to each other, ignoring the superintendent. " Why would Hawk want Major dead? They were friends."

" Major knew things about the murders, " said Wren. "Without him, it weakens our ability to form a case against him."

"What does he care? We have him for murder. You and I both watched him shoot Karen Freeman in the head. He's going to be locked up for life regardless. You don't think he thinks he can wriggle out of this?"

Wren spread her hands. " People sometimes get out on parole on a single murder charge. It happens."

" Bastard," said Reilly. " That … " He looked at Wren. Touched the bandage on his face. "Sorry. I shouldn't call him that."

"It's fine," said Wren. "You're not wrong."

"This isn't going to stop us," said Reilly. "We'll find the evidence we need to tie it to him. Besides, you said he confessed to you out there. So, you're a witness."

"Yeah," said Wren. "And I'm not the least bit biased."

Reilly sighed.

The superintendent spoke up. " I really am very sorry about this. It's not often that inmates find ways to harm themselves here. It really is a safe facility."

"We don't blame you," said Reilly. "We'll see ourselves out."

They left the jail and went out to the parking lot, where they got into Wren's car. She insisted on driving until Reilly was fully recovered. He agreed, but only — he said — because he didn't want her to make more comments about his masculinity if he argued with her.

Reilly sat down in the passenger seat and yanked the

seatbelt on. "Is it, uh, is it too soon to ask you about why Hawk did all of this?"

She looked at him, considering. Then she turned away. "Yeah. A little too soon."

* * *

Natalie was sitting on a park bench, clutching a stuffed teddy bear. Her sister Jessica was on her feet, gazing longingly at the swing set, but it was clear she wasn't going anywhere without her sister.

The girls might have been too old for playgrounds. Maybe other girls their age would rather play with apps on their phones and experiment with makeup, but Natalie and Jessica were making up for lost time. They'd never seen playgrounds before coming out of the woods. They were enamored with swings and slides, or so Wren had been told by their new foster mother, a woman named Lori.

Lori seemed like a nice enough woman, and she had agreed for Wren to take the girls on an outing. The girls were apparently excited at the prospect, considering Wren was someone vaguely familiar in this new world they inhabited. When she'd shown up at the door, they had both smiled at her, big smiles, and taken her to their bedroom to show her all their new clothes and their stuffed animals and toys.

Lori had suggested Wren take them to the playground.

Now, they were here, but the girls weren't playing.

Natalie gripped her teddy even tighter.

"Do you want to go back home?" Wren said.

Natalie turned to her sharply. "Can you take us there?"

Wren's mouth suddenly went dry, realizing her mistake. The girls still thought of their house in the woods as home. They missed it, and they missed their parents. No matter how dysfunctional their lives had been before, the girls didn't know any differently. "I'm sorry," she said. "You can't go back there."

"I told you," Jessica said, giving Natalie an annoyed look.

"There wouldn't be anyone there to take care of us."

"Maybe Wren could take care of us," said Natalie.

"Me?" Wren touched her chest. "Um, look, I'm not…"

"Wren doesn't want to live in the woods," said Jessica, folding her arms over her chest. "She doesn't want to live without electricity and running water and toilets."

Natalie scrunched up her face. "The showers *are* nice," she conceded.

"Exactly," said Jessica.

"I thought you liked Lori," said Wren. "She's nice, isn't she?"

Natalie nodded. "She's nice."

"She's really nice," said Jessica. "You want to go on the swings?"

"I can push you guys," said Wren. "Or we can all swing. We can have a contest to see who can swing the highest."

"Lori's nice, but she's not Mom," said Natalie. "I miss Mom."

Jessica looked down at her feet.

"Of course you do," said Wren. "You'll always miss her."

"Always?" said Natalie.

Wren nodded. "Always." And then she wondered what the hell she was saying. She should say something that would cheer Natalie up. Natalie needed hope now, not the grim, sad truth. But she couldn't think of anything to say.

"Mom would be happy for us," said Jessica in a quiet voice. "Remember how she always told us that she wasn't going to let us be in the woods forever?"

"But Dad said—"

"But Mom was going to get us out of there," said Jessica. "She'd be here with us if she could."

"She would," Wren agreed, even though the girls' mother, were she alive, would probably be in jail for murder. Police had searched the area around the pavilion, and they had identified the bones of four different men, all of whom had gone missing over the past fifteen years. Karen had participated. She wasn't innocent. That, however, was something Wren didn't feel the need to share with the girls. "She'd want you to enjoy all the things you can enjoy out here."

"Like swings," said Jessica, holding out her hand to her sister. "Come on."

Natalie took a deep breath. "Well, okay. That contest sounds fun." She smiled at Wren.

"Let's do it," said Wren, grinning back.

The three headed for the swings.

As Wren pumped her legs at the sky, and the girls giggled next to her, she felt good, an expansive feeling somewhere in her chest. It brought tears to her eyes too, for some reason.

She didn't know why she was here, why she'd sought these girls out. But for some reason, she couldn't stop thinking about them. She had thought that she only wanted to make sure the girls were okay, but she and Lori had already spoken about her visiting the girls on a semi-regular basis. She wanted to be part of these girls lives. She didn't know why, but it felt right.

***

Reilly waved at Timmy, who was coming out of the building at school.

When Timmy saw him, his eyes lit up and he took off at run for Reilly.

Reilly grinned, and he had to admit he was really, really relieved. He and Janessa had not been sure this would work. Timmy was used to his mother picking him up from school. Reilly doing it instead could easily be disastrous, and he had steeled himself for picking Timmy up off the ground while the little boy had a screaming meltdown.

Timmy arrived next to the car, a little out of breath, his eyes shining. "Thomas pulled into Knapford Yard to see his friend Percy waiting for him. Thomas and Percy were best friends."

Reilly's eyes stung. "Hey, buddy. You're my best friend too. Is it okay that I'm picking you up from school instead of your mom?"

"Is it okay," said Timmy. "Is it okay."

Reilly took this as assent. "You want to get in the car?"

"Get in the car." Timmy was bouncing up and down.

Reilly opened the door and Timmy crawled inside. Reilly helped him buckle his seatbelt and then he went to the front of the car. "Well, we're going to go home and we can play all weekend."

"We can play," said Timmy. "We can *play!*"

"Yeah, whatever you want," said Reilly, glancing up at him in the rear view mirror. He started the car. "I got some more of those puzzles you like. We can put them together."

"Bust my buffers," said Timmy.

Reilly chuckled. "We can also put train tracks together, if you want."

"If you want," said Timmy. "If I want."

Reilly's eyebrows shot up. "What did you just say?"

"What did you just say. What did you just say. What did I just say."

Reilly let out a disbelieving laugh. "You just said 'I.' You changed the pronoun, buddy. You did that all by yourself."

"All by yourself."

"Timmy did it all by himself."

"Timmy did it. Timmy did it." Timmy was bouncing the back seat, looking pleased with himself.

Reilly pulled the car out of the parking lot, and he was so full of hope for his little son, that he thought he might burst.

CHAPTER THIRTY-TWO

Wren took a deep breath, and then she picked up the phone in the visitor area at the prison. On the other side of the glass, Vivian Delacroix already had the phone to her ear. She was smiling like a satisfied cat. Wren half-expected to hear her purr through the receiver.

"I'm so glad you changed your mind," said Vivian. "I've wanted to reconnect with you for a long time. For too long."

"That's not what this is," Wren said, giving Vivian a level gaze. "We're not reconnecting."

"No? Come on, Wren, it's okay to admit that you've missed me. I'm your mother, after all, and I love you. I know that not having you in my life has been like living with a hole in my heart."

"Save it," said Wren. "I'm not interested."

"I don't see why you'd bother to come here if you didn't want to talk to me."

"I want answers," said Wren.

"You have questions?"

Wren looked away, placing her splayed fingers on the ledge in front of her. "No, I don't have questions. That's not it, actually. I have the answers. I'm only here because I want you to know that I know."

"That you know what?" said Vivian.

Wren licked her lips. "I was about eight years old. Maybe seven. I can't remember exactly. It's funny that way, because I remember other things about it really vividly. I can remember almost everything you said, and what Dad said back—"

"I don't mean to interrupt," said Vivian, "but that thing you said before about Adrian Campbell? You don't really think he's your father, do you?"

Wren looked up at Vivian sharply. "What?"

Vivian laughed, and she looked as though she was having a very good time. "If you want to know who your father *really* is, then—"

"No," Wren snapped. "We're not playing that game." But this did explain why she hadn't been a bone marrow match for Emmaline Campbell, if it was true. She'd gotten the phone call a few days ago, and the doctor told her that they'd already notified Emmaline and her family. Wren had thought about calling them. She'd wanted to call. But she hadn't. She hadn't known what to say.

Now, she realized that it all could have been a smokescreen by Vivian. She'd tried to extort money from Adrian, but that didn't mean he was really Wren's biological father. Wren felt something inside her rip free again, and it hurt. Damn Vivian.

"All I want from you is a relationship, Wren, sweetheart. Is that too much to ask?"

"You don't want a relationship with me," said Wren, glaring at her. "You don't give a flying fuck about me. This memory I have? I remember what you said. You and Dad were arguing, because he was leaving the compound to go and work during the day, and I was left in your care, and you were annoyed about having to look after me. It was summer time, and I wasn't in school, and having me underfoot was making you crazy."

"Oh, any mother has felt that from time to time," said Vivian. "I don't know why you're bringing this up."

"You said, 'I can't be bothered with looking out for the brat all the time. If you care so much, you quit your job and corral her.'"

"Maybe I did," said Vivian. "I was frazzled and

overwhelmed. I was practically running the entire FCL at that point. David had retreated to his little mansion, and I had to deal with the day-to-day. I hardly had time for your knee scrapes."

"You said, 'I don't think I was meant to be a mother. I don't think it's in me. I told you this when I was pregnant. I wanted to get rid of it, but you convinced me that you would shoulder the parenting responsibilities.' And Dad said, 'She nearly broke her arm.' Which is funny, because I don't remember nearly breaking my arm. I don't remember anything about that. I remember that I was supposed to be asleep, but that you two were talking too loudly, and so I heard everything. You said, 'I wish she would have broken her neck. Then I'd have one less thing to worry about.'"

"Oh, Lord, Wren, I didn't mean that."

"See, I think you did," Wren said. "You're good at fooling most people, but you don't fool me. I see you, just like I see other criminals. It's why I'm so good at profiling. I understand. Sure, you're right, most women get frustrated being a mother. They may have moments in which they wish they'd never had children. But they love their children more than they love themselves. And you don't do that. You don't love anything at all. Only yourself."

"You're being melodramatic and—"

"You're good at pretending to be like other people, but you're not like them."

"Wren, darling, I'm sorry that what I said hurt you. You should never have heard me say something like that. I swear, I didn't mean it. I do love you. More than anything on earth. You're my one and only daughter. You must believe—"

"I don't," said Wren. "I know that you don't love. You get interested in other people as a sort of mind experiment, a challenge to yourself to see how far you can dominate them, what you can push them to do. In your mind, the world in your chessboard, and everyone in it is just a piece for you to figure out how to move around. Your only amusement comes from subjugating others and the further you can push them, the better."

"You're being horrible." Vivian drew herself up. "I won't tolerate being spoken to this way. I'm your mother."

"I used to think you used the acid to make people more susceptible," said Wren. "But then I realized that didn't make any sense. For one thing, you like a challenge. And for another, someone told me that acid makes you feel connected to every living thing, so that it's harder to be violent on hallucinogens than it is normally. That's when I realized you did it because you liked it when other people felt connected with you. I don't think you felt connected with them, though. I don't think even the effects of hallucinogens made you care. I think it only brought it into sharper relief the difference between yourself and other people. You saw how they connected to each other, and you realized you'd never feel that way. I think it made you feel more lonely."

"Wren, darling…" Vivian swallowed. "I don't have any idea what you're talking about. Everyone was doing drugs back there. We thought it was spiritual."

"You *are* lonely, aren't you?" said Wren, gazing deep into her mother's eyes. "Always lonely. Because no matter what, you never find anyone like you. Only weak people, people who break easily when you try to manipulate them. There is no one else worthy of you."

"I'm lonely because I'm in prison," said Vivian and now there was an edge to her voice. "Honestly, if you only came here to taunt me—"

"So, what you decided to do was to use the LSD to try to make people more like you," said Wren. "When they were tripping, they were open to you, connected to you, and you flooded them with your mind view—that murder was glorious and holy, and your nightmarish descriptions of the Crimson Ram. You tried to turn them into you."

"I have no idea what you're going on about. If this is all

you're going to say to me, then I'm going to hang up and leave."

"No, you're not. You're bored. I'm more entertaining than anything in your cell, even if you're annoyed by the fact you can't manipulate me. Actually, that makes me more interesting. I'm a challenge."

Vivian pressed her lips together. She didn't say anything.

"You had some success," said Wren. "Certainly, the fact that you got Garrett and Lexi and Karen and Terrence to kill, that was your triumph. You convinced them only with your words and with the god you created. But they weren't really like you, because they had regrets. In the end, they had so much regret that they betrayed you and turned you in. You pushed and pushed and pushed. But the Walker Massacre ended up being a bridge too far. You got in over your head. Experiment failed."

"I…" Vivian sniffed. "I didn't fail at anything."

Wren chuckled dryly. "Ooh, I should have known that would get under your skin. But you had another experiment, didn't you? Two boys. See, usually, you wouldn't give kids hallucinogens. I don't know why. Maybe some shred of decency inside you? Maybe something else? But there was an exception, and that was Hawk and Major. You sent them out with the others, you fed them mushrooms and acid, and you got in their heads."

"Did I?" Vivian raised both of her eyebrows.

"That experiment was successful," said Wren. "Eventually successful, anyway. At the time, I think you thought it failed."

"I don't know where you're getting this." Vivian shrugged.

"Hawk told me that the Crimson Ram had plans for me, but that you wanted me to be safe, and that was why you got us paired together, so that he could protect me. But I thought about that, and the only way anyone knew about the Crimson Ram's plans was through you, because you made them up. So, I was never in danger. You convinced Hawk that the Horned Lord wanted him to kill me. And then you pretended that you didn't want that, because no mother really wants her daughter murdered. Except you did. I was an annoyance and you wanted me out of the way. If Hawk would kill me, it got rid of your aggravation and it also demonstrated your dominance over him. You were molding him to your own will, turning him into you, another version of you."

Vivian sat back in her chair, holding the phone to her ear. She coolly regarded Wren.

"He didn't kill me," said Wren. "He protected me. But whatever you did to him, it got in his head, and he couldn't stop hearing the Horned Lord telling him to kill me. So, he killed other girls. And when that didn't shut up the voice, he tried to kill to protect me, but that didn't work either. You were deep in there. You had wormed your way all the way inside him. Remade him from the inside out."

"Are you trying to blame me for someone else's crimes?" murmured Vivian. "You always did have a crush on Hawk."

"No, I lay blame at his feet," said Wren. "You may have whispered in his ear, but he did the deeds. There are no excuses for the things he did. That's not what I'm doing here. I'm not excusing. I'm explaining."

"Does it make you feel better to explain his behavior?"

"Sometimes." Wren took a deep breath. "I understand that compulsive feeling he has, that need he has to kill me. See, I'm compulsive too. I have this need to figure you out, Vivian, and no matter what I unravel about you and about other killers like you, it's never enough. You whispered in my ear too. I'm stronger than Hawk. I would never hurt little girls. But that doesn't mean you didn't royally fuck me up too. So, thanks for that, Mom." She hung up the phone and blew a kiss at the glass.

Vivian leaned forward, saying something, but Wren couldn't make it out.

She stood up and turned her back on Vivian.
Slowly and deliberately, she walked away.

Manufactured by Amazon.ca
Bolton, ON